COYOTE IN THE MOUNTAINS
AND OTHER STORIES

For Corine

—Place you'll Recognize

BY JOHN REMBER
ILLUSTRATION BY JULIE SCOTT

John Rember

LIMBERLOST PRESS 1989

ACKNOWLEDGEMENTS: Each of these stories, some in slight-ly altered versions, appeared in different editions of the *Idaho Mountain Express*.

I.S.B.N. 0-931659-05-1

This book is published by Limberlost Press, Rick and Rosemary Ardinger, Editors, HC 33, Box 1113, Boise, Idaho 83706.

For Sandy

CONTENTS

A Few Beers and a Road Trip   3

Loonatic   15

A Small Get-together   25

Object Lessons   39

User Friendly   51

The Bright Beauty of the World   65

Visiting Rabbit   75

Coyote in Love   89

Coyote in the Mountains   99

A FEW BEERS
AND A ROAD TRIP

COYOTE, IN PREPARATION FOR A JOURNEY, began to clean his car. It was not a small task. He had avoided it until a series of warm spring days had melted the pad of ice which built up on the floorboards during the winter. Things frozen there had escaped. A rich malignant smell hung about the vehicle, a smell compounded of spilled beer, hamburger wrappers, and the disintegrating contents of forgotten doggie bags.

Coyote armed himself with a plastic bucket and a garden trowel and began scraping material from under the seat into the bucket. He poked at a mound of green claws, which on inspection turned into an envelope of lost french fries. What a relief, he thought, remembering the medieval doctrine of spontaneous generation, the idea that new life came wriggling out of the decay of the old. Who could say what strange creatures would arise from the sediment of his journeys, would come out of the floorboard muck and slip wet tentacles around his ankles as he drove?

In the back seat he found pieces of clothing he had been missing for months, overdue library books, uncashed checks, unpaid bills, and a Publisher's Clearinghouse Sweepstakes million-dollar envelope, stamped, ready to go, its deadline long passed. He went over the interior of the car with a vacuum, watching, fascinated, as newness seeped back into the upholstery behind the wand. Magic, he thought. Renewal. Lengthening afternoons. For a moment, he thought he caught a trace of new car smell, gone a hundred thousand miles ago.

He began wiping the dust off the dashboard with a towel, erasing old phone numbers, times of appointments, and the license numbers of cars which had beaten him to parking spaces. He hesitated only a little over the last, realizing his plans to look up the owners and knock out their windshields with a baseball bat were more trouble than they were worth. Let someone else be the agent of karma, he thought, and swept the cracked vinyl clean.

He washed the car and stepped back and looked at it. Its color scheme was working toward pinto, its tires were bald, and he had left most of its grille in a snowbank a winter or two before. But it still looked like it would travel, and the mountain landscape behind it, a chocolate sundae mess of melting snow and mud, suggested it should.

He was still standing there, contemplating destinations, when his neighbor Badger stepped up behind him.

"Road trip," said Badger.

"I think so," said Coyote.

"Where to?"

Coyote said he didn't know.

Badger walked in front of him and inspected the car. "You want company?" he asked.

Coyote frowned. Badger was not always safe to travel with. He held radical political views and expressed them to strangers in red-and-black wool jackets. He made fun of local high school teams in cafes that displayed their athletic calendars. He talked about what would happen after the Revolution, but never got to the paradise stage, preferring instead to concentrate on images of fat cats hanging from lamp posts. A few hours after he hit a city, he could be found in a bar that played classical music on its stereo, talking Marx and feminism, looking for girls in wire-rim glasses and work-shirts. One of them, a long time ago, had embroidered a North Vietnamese flag on the back of Badger's Levi jacket. Coyote caught himself staring at its time-bleached colors.

"Sure," he said. "Come on along. Get your stuff."

A few minutes later, as Coyote was loading his backpack and

sleeping bag into the back seat, Badger appeared, dragging a large duffel and carrying a case of beer under one arm.

"Wait," said Badger. "We need food." He ran madly back into his house, returning with a family-size bag of corn chips and several cans of refried bean dip.

A mile or so later, as they headed south and down on the only road out of the mountains, Badger finished his first beer. He rolled down his window, and, taking aim at a CAUTION sign on the roadside, pegged the empty bottle into it. Glass exploded back toward the road, hitting the pavement behind the car.

"Nice shot," said Coyote.

"Where we going, anyway?"

"Someplace with green grass," said Coyote.

"So where?"

"Lower altitudes. Higher temperatures. I want to feel warm ground under my bare feet."

Badger barked a laugh. "That's the way you get hookworm," he said.

In a little while they crossed the line between mountain and desert. Patches of snow gradually gave way to the solid grey and black of sage and lava rock.

Badger reached for the bag of corn chips and spilled them across the seats and floor. He began grinding them to bits with his boots. "We need some females," he said. "All road trips need some."

"Any particular kind?" asked Coyote.

"Proletariat females, preferably. Strong young daughters of the working class. Factory girls. Oppressed secretaries."

Coyote remarked that where they were going, the towns had been born out of desert valleys, irrigation, and religious fervor, and the closest things to factories were Mormon Churches and Arctic Circle drive-ins.

"Let's start with the Arctic Circles," said Badger.

They continued south. Periodically, Badger would open the window, letting in a blast of cold spring air and throwing a beer bottle into a billboard.

"You should have tried out for the majors," said Coyote.

Badger turned and glared at him. "Major league baseball," he said, "is one of the ways the ruling classes in this country keep slaves from waking up. Baseball and movie stars. Mother's Day. Health clubs. Vulgar foreign cars. They all stop you from thinking."

He gestured at the cracked faces of dashboard gauges. "Now this car. This car you can think in. No digital displays to hypnotize you. No electronic voice saying, 'You're a better person than your neighbor who doesn't have a new car. Work hard and some day you can afford another new one.' What you have here is an honest proletarian road-trip vehicle."

"It took me years to get it like this," said Coyote.

Badger had once gone on a road trip to Chicago, not as a hot prospect for the Cubs bullpen, but as a demonstrator at the 1968 Democratic Convention. There he had been tear-gassed and had his skull fractured by a Chicago policeman. He had spent the rest of a long hot summer in and out of surgical wards.

He hadn't been the same since. It was as if all the subtle shadings of his memory had been erased by a nightstick. In their place were the enormous facts of a cop, a club, the breaking of bones in his head and jaw. This was the context into which Badger had placed all subsequent experience.

He feared and hated anyone wearing a uniform. He claimed to see direct connections between police and high-school cheerleaders, UPS drivers, bellhops, even the teen-aged candystripers in the hospitals he had stayed in. He became a rabid judge of American consumer society, pronouncing those with ranch-style mortgages, console TV's, pre-purchased burial plots and rising expectations to be slimy bourgeois grubs that fed on the rotten core of the the capitalist system. In his back pocket he carried an antique copy of Mao's Little Red Book.

Sometime after the Viet Nam War ended, Badger began running into people who didn't know what the flag on his jacket stood for. Former radicals became apostles of the insurance industry. *Rolling Stone* magazine, having successfully told America what the Altamont Raceway Rock Festival was all about, began to tell America about the heroics of new-wave entrepreneurs and the wonders of new-age electronics. Then apocryphal stories began popping up about young girls who didn't know Paul McCartney had been in another band before Wings. In the face of it all, Badger kept a steady faith, refreshing himself by means of occasional encounters with rural deputy sheriffs who hadn't been through sensitivity training.

Badger rolled down his window and pitched out a bottle. His target was a litter barrel at a roadside turn-out, and the bottle sailed into the barrel without touching the rim.

"Maybe you should have tried out for the Celtics," said Coyote.

At that moment Coyote noticed flashing lights in his rearview mirror. He pulled over. A state trooper got out of the car behind him and walked up to Coyote's window.

"I saw that," said the trooper.

Coyote nodded. "Good, isn't he?"

"Pig," said Badger. "Fascist."

The trooper bent down to look at Badger. Then he looked at Coyote. "Can I see your license?"

"May," said Badger. "That's, 'May I see your license? Please.'"

Coyote handed over his driver's license. The trooper began writing something down in his ticket book.

"Why don't you go back to El Salvador where you belong?" yelled Badger. "Your buddies on the death squad are missing you."

The trooper continued writing. "Been drinking?" he asked.

Badger belched.

Coyote had to blow up a little balloon to prove he was sober. When this was done, the trooper handed him back his license and said, "I have a citation all filled out. I'm going to be right behind you. If either of you throw anything out of this car, if you miss a turn signal, if a bolt falls off or some more paint peels off, I'm going to bust your ass. Understand?"

Coyote nodded.

"After the Revolution, fella," said Badger, "You're going to be working for us."

Coyote rested his head on the steering wheel.

"Where'd you dig him up, anyway?" asked the trooper.

"Half his skull's a stainless steel plate," said Coyote. "Viet Nam."

"Oh," said the cop. "You should have said something."

"We just take care of him," said Coyote. "We don't advertise him."

"Sorry," the trooper said. He tore the ticket out of his book and crumpled it up. "I went in after the Tet Offensive. What a mess."

"Yeah," said Coyote.

"Don't let him throw any more bottles out the window," said the trooper, and walked back to his car.

"Pig," said Badger. "Lackey. Hired killer." He spoke in a low voice and only Coyote heard him.

"Why'd you tell him that?" asked Badger as Coyote rolled up his window. "Why'd you tell him I've got a plate in my head?"

"Because you do."

"Why'd you say I got it in Viet Nam?"

"I didn't say you got it in Viet Nam. I just said Viet Nam. If it wasn't for Viet Nam you wouldn't have a plate in your head, would you?"

"At least I didn't go there," Badger said. He fell into a sullen silence.

Coyote shrugged. He had joined up in 1967, putting a check mark beside HELICOPTERS because he had always wanted to fly. They had made him a door gunner. He had spent his hitch on the Mekong Delta, flying high-speed night runs a few feet off the surface of canals and rivers, blowing sampans out of the water with a machine gun. He had been through his war without really knowing if he'd killed anyone, never seeing again the little boats that sank into the night behind the searchlight glare.

Sometimes someone had shot back. Holes appeared in the fuselage beside him, bits of rotor spattered into his face, stinging but not drawing blood. He was never wounded. He went through three ships in a year, and twice watched as pilots he had walked and talked with a few hours earlier burned in wreckage. He was always picked up by rescue craft, always sent out again. And always it had the air of dream about it, the feeling it was happening to someone else. He had never been in Viet Nam the way Badger had been in Chicago.

It's just as well, he thought, watching as Badger finished yet another beer, moodily rolled down the window and hooked the empty bottle into the back of a pickup passing in the opposite direction. Coyote looked in the rear-view mirror for the police cruiser. It was a small dot on the horizon.

"I think you should quit that," said Coyote.

"Go to hell," said Badger. He rolled up his window, leaned against it and closed his eyes. Coyote, worried that Badger might fall out, leaned over him and locked his door.

Bits of grass began to show along the roadside. Ahead, Coyote could see fields of winter wheat, their color a shocking green. And beyond them, he could see a town, marked by its water tower, the spire of its church, and the greenish-grey of trees coming into leaf. As they came closer, Coyote made out the flickering neon ice-cream-cone of a drive-in restaurant.

Badger was snoring softly when Coyote parked the car beside the drive-in's dumpster.

"We're here," said Coyote. "R and R port." Badger did not move. Coyote got out of the car, stopped, reached back in through the steering wheel for the keys, crossed the gravel parking lot to the drive-in, went in and sat down.

"How are your hamburgers?" he asked the high-school girl who appeared across the counter from him.

"They're all right if you eat them before they set up," she said.

Fair enough, thought Coyote. He ordered one for himself and one for Badger. He swiveled his stool around so he faced the sun coming through the windows.

He sat motionless for what seemed like a long time, then turned around when he heard the girl behind him.

"You want anything with these?" she asked, handing him two stained paper bags, the burgers heavy inside, their outlines recognizable through the paper.

"No." He paid her. "Did you know Paul McCartney was in another band before Wings?" he asked her.

"Who's Paul McCartney?" she asked.

He smiled at her. "Just somebody who used to be important."

He walked back to the car, opened his door and tossed one of the burger bags onto Badger's lap. Badger opened his eyes.

"We there yet?" he asked.

"I don't know," said Coyote. "I'll check." He reached and turned on the radio and dialed it to a local station he had seen advertised on a billboard outside of town. Country music pounded from the speaker. He took off his shoes and walked gingerly around to the front of the car. He threw his burger on the hood and climbed up after it, and was amazed at the hot paint beneath him. He leaned back against the windshield.

"This is really living," he said.

"Huhnmmm?" said Badger, his mouth full.

"This is really living," he said, shouting through the glass.

"You're easily amused," said Badger.

Coyote sat back and bit into the burger, realizing with a quick pang of regret that he should have gotten to it sooner. At least he wouldn't have to eat for a day or so.

The bass notes of the music penetrated to his bones. He could see the girl behind the glass of the drive-in window.

"Do you realize," he said, looking between elbow and ribs at Badger, "that for as long as this world exists, there will be high-school girls working in drive-ins every spring? Saving money for

10

college? Waiting to get off shift so they can meet their boyfriends?"

Badger turned off the radio. He looked grey and unhealthy underneath the tint of the windshield. "What?" he asked.

"Nothing," said Coyote. He realized he could go home now. It was odd it had taken so little—a greasy hamburger, a girl in a drive-in restaurant, bright clean air between the toes, Dolly Parton on the radio. These things grounded you in the world, proved that for all its delicacy, it still really did exist. Badger was right, he thought. I am easily amused.

He finished the burger. He squeezed the bag into a ball, dropped it, and watched as a breeze tumbled it off the hood onto the ground.

"Litterbug," screamed Badger.

"Time to go back," said Coyote. He got in and started the engine. He drove slowly out of the parking lot and headed north, up into the snow again.

Badger scowled. "This wasn't much of a road trip," he said.

"I just needed to get someplace," said Coyote.

Badger snorted. "Did you get there?"

Coyote didn't answer. He reached into the half-empty case of beer and pulled out a bottle and opened it. A few minutes later he pulled out another one.

Miles later, after the grass had disappeared and the snowbanks were deepening along the road edge, Coyote drove at high speed through the centers of puddles, tossed bottles at the white lines, and made obscene gestures at police cars in the opposite lane. He found an ancient Janis Joplin tape in the glove compartment, jammed it into the tape deck, and cranked it up. And all the time, so that Badger could have a springtime too, Coyote pretended it was 1968.

LOONATIC

ONE BRIGHT MORNING Coyote sat in the sun on his front porch and drank six cups of coffee. Then he walked out to his mailbox. There was a caffeine spring in his step, and had he been asked if coffee made him tense and irritable, he would have replied no, it made him tense and happy. No coffee companies had called for endorsements but he was ready to recommend the product if asked. Most mornings, he would say, if it's warm and you don't have a dental appointment or a funeral to go to, caffeine is the ingestible substance of choice.

In his mailbox he found a letter from Loon. A time capsule, he thought. It had been five years since he had heard from Loon, the last contact coming as a phone call in the middle of the night.

"You think you can get away with it, don't you?" Loon had asked.

"Huh?" Coyote had been sleeping soundly and had not been sure whom he was talking to, or even where he was.

"You smart guys," Loon screamed over the phone. "You think you're going to be young and beautiful forever. Let me tell you something. It doesn't happen that way."

"Who is this?"

"Real life is going to catch up with you sooner or later."

"Loon?"

There was a short silence on the other end of the line.

"Yeah."

"Where are you?"

"In a phone booth. They took us on a field trip. I got away."

"You all right?"

"No," Loon had giggled. "Still crazy."

"I'm sorry to hear that."

"It's not your fault. Anyway, it isn't so bad. I get my own room at the hospital. I paint things. Portraits."

"You'll have to send me something for the walls."

"I've been painting my neighbor. I'm calling it 'Still Life with Doctor.'"

"What?"

"He's catatonic. During psychotherapy he doesn't even blink."

"Oh," said Coyote.

"I just wanted to warn you about being young and beautiful. Nothing lasts forever."

"It doesn't?"

"It was a shock to me too, when I found out," Loon said, and hung up.

Coyote had spent the rest of the night drifting through bad dreams, waking now and then to wonder if Loon really had been painting his catatonic ward-mate, sneaking out of bed at night and covering the fellow with green and orange day-glo stripes, sneaking back before the orderlies made their morning rounds.

The return address on the envelope surprised him. Loon had sent it from a small town a few hours away, in a volcanic part of the state. Coyote had hung out there once—it was the hometown of an old lover—and he remembered that it had been bordered by irrigated fields on one side and lava flows on another. Its main street was cut off at one end by a colossal cinder cone. In the recent geological past, the place had been molten. A river on a third edge of town had cut down through the layers of older lava flows until it had created a huge, vertical-walled canyon. The streets running toward it ended in catastrophe. One could do well in the insurance industry there, he had thought, selling fire, automobile, and life policies by pointing a finger at the appropriate hazard.

It didn't seem a wise place for Loon to move.

Coyote stood on his front porch and opened the envelope. Inside was a photograph. Nothing else. It was of Loon standing in a suburban back yard. There was a gas barbeque, and a hammock tied between a white painted fence and a small tree. A picnic table and chairs were scattered about on the grass. Loon's face dominated the photo. Its eyes were focused on something far behind the camera. Beyond Loon and the short expanse of yard there was nothing. Empty space. The back yard ended at the edge of the abyss.

Coyote peered again at the return address. He walked to his car, got in, started the engine, then shut it off and walked back into his house. He returned with a full cup of coffee. He started his car and drove out of the yard, toward a distant junction of highways.

Coyote leaned back against the seat, and settled in for a leisurely trip. A few miles later he looked at the speedometer, saw he was going ninety miles an hour, and slowed to seventy-five. No hurry, he thought, but then watched as the needle crawled back up to ninety. Things felt better at ninety. They really did. He grinned down the highway, wondering what speed Loon was feeling comfortable at these days.

There had been a time Loon had traveled light-years in seconds. Shortly before he had been carted away, Loon had invited Coyote to his house. He had been waiting out front when Coyote had come up the walk.

"I have something really important to show you," Loon said.

"I don't want to see any Amway movies," said Coyote.

Loon had pulled him through the front door. The interior of the house was dark. With a start, Coyote realized the lights were on. Loon had painted the walls, floors, ceiling, furniture and fixtures a dull black. Here and there on the wall nearest him were small glittering things. He walked over to one and saw it was a tiny portrait of a star.

Further into the house, Loon had painted great spiral galaxies on the walls, dusty nebulae on the ceiling, the drifting wisps of comets on the tables and chairs. In the dining room, on what had once been a picture window, a huge red sun stood out from the blackness. A hundred or so planets surrounded it, and a thousand half-lit moons surrounded the planets.

"This is my starship," Loon had told him. Then, gesturing around at his house, he said, "Welcome to my space."

"Where'd you put all the black holes?" Coyote had asked, as a joke.

Loon had turned to him, a terrible recognition on his face. "Oh," he said. "Oh, God, no." He grabbed at a wall switch and turned out the lights.

It had been real, Coyote thought several days later, after he had calmed down. The small stars had been bright points suspended in emptiness, the nebulae had been dim glows parsecs above him. Too near, the great red sun had cast its light on its satellites, making them into so many orbiting hells. Loon had used phosphorescent paint.

"Black holes," Loon screamed in the darkness. "I didn't even think about the black holes."

Coyote had run for the door, barking his shin on a coffee table on the way, tripping over a chair after that. He got up, clawed for the door handle, finally found it and let himself out into the world.

Loon's neighbors, after listening to whimpers and howls for a night, had called the police. Loon had been found gibbering in a corner, some essential part of him disappeared, sucked beyond an internal event horizon.

So I said the wrong thing, Coyote had thought later. How was he to know what Loon's starship had meant to him, what coming to terms with the universe the black hole question had doomed? Nobody said it was going to be safe out there.

The highway Coyote turned onto cut straight through a lava field. On either side of his car Coyote could see piles of ragged cinders, their blackness softened only by spots of lichen and an occasional motel or restaurant billboard, its bleached paper peeling away to display the ad of an older and defunct business. Nothing did last forever, he thought. Loon's call from the hospital had been rational enough in that respect. Judging from Coyote's face in his bathroom mirror on some recent mornings, Loon had been right about the truth and beauty, too.

A hundred miles later, the lava smoothed out and became farm. Coyote passed a speed limit sign, slowed to thirty-five, and watched impatiently as the car crawled past fences and driveways. He discovered that fences were made up of individual posts. He made eye contact with horses in fields.

Farmland gave way to a raw subdivision where the mailboxes came in clusters and the trees were staked upright. Pastel houses went by at regularly spaced intervals. Daffodils bloomed in front of a few of them. Coyote wondered if Loon had driven by, and if he had seen the flowers or only what they stood for. A single rose could be a dangerous idea, he knew from experience. God only knew what mad metaphors the daffodils had sparked in Loon's brain.

Without warning, the highway became the main street of town. Mature trees obscured houses with lava-rock foundations. Painted signs staked into front lawns advertised hair-care or gunsmithing operations. Sidewalks began, and with them the business district. Beyond the theater marquee, the Ford dealer's sign, the insurance and real-estate agencies and the Safeway, Coyote could see the vast truncated cone of the volcano, its black sides covered with white painted numbers marking the graduating years of fifty high-school classes. Ruts made by four-wheel-drive vehicles stretched nearly to its summit. A more reverent people, he thought, would still be keeping the secret of its name, praying to it, and telling legends of a time when it had gotten angry.

He watched a girl walk down the sidewalk toward him. He waved at her. She waved back and smiled, each gesture a gift. Her ass swayed in his rear-view mirror. Now, he thought, there's something that could drive you crazy.

At the base of the volcano he turned left toward the canyon. Ahead of him, two blocks away, the road ended raggedly, marked by two signs covered with yellow and black diagonal stripes. Between them there was a row of small steel posts, and between the posts was strung a cable. It was not a reassuring barrier. Local suicides blew through it all the time. At the next intersection Coyote tested his brakes, grateful, for once, for a stop sign.

He held the photograph Loon had sent him on his lap, and as he turned and drove parallel to the canyon he checked its perspective of the far wall with his own. It was not a road map, but it worked. In a few minutes, he stopped in front of the house where Loon had been.

It was empty. Gaping holes showed where the front windows had been pulled out. The front door was gone. Coyote walked across the yard and into the living room. Nothing had been painted black, to his relief, but light fixtures had been torn off the ceiling, carpet had been ripped up, and the railing of a stairway was gone. Anything that could be moved was not there. In the kitchen he found the marks of a refrigerator and a stove on the linoleum, and a hole where the sink had been. He stepped through another open doorway to the back yard.

Nothing was left. There was no picnic table, no barbeque. The hammock was gone, and so was the fence it had been tied to. So was the tree. Its stump, marked by hundreds of hatchet hacks, suggested a boy scout on angel dust.

He walked to the edge and looked over. It was all down there, the refrigerator, stove, window frames, beds, barbeque and the rest of it, littering the rocks at the base of the canyon wall, looking like pieces from a doll's house. There was a car down there too, its back window starred and opaque, and the folded remains of a trailer house. He turned to look for tire tracks and found them, faint flattenings of the grass on the edge, leading backwards through the narrow strip connecting the front and back yards. He looked over the edge again. It was a long way straight down.

He studied the photograph. Loon looked out of it and through him. He would have liked to have asked Loon what he had been looking at, who had held the camera, and what shapes had lurched toward him from the horizon.

He flipped the photo out into the air over the canyon, and watched it glide and tumble and fall until it went out of sight, still far above the canyon floor. It was as though it had never existed. He imagined Loon, finally released from the mental hospital, casually throwing a rock or bottle or spent aerosol can over the edge, watching it fall until it winked into nothingness.

That would have done it, thought Coyote, remembering from a new perspective Loon's claim that nothing lasted forever. For Loon, nothing did last forever. It swallowed everything he threw into it, no matter how much he threw or how big an object was thrown. Coyote supposed that Loon, his consciousness squeezed to a point of incomprehensible singularity, had been trying to fill up the canyon.

Coyote walked back to his car, drove under the late afternoon shadow of the volcano, and turned again onto the main street. These people must lack imagination, he told himself. Otherwise they wouldn't live here.

He stopped at a cafe, bought a paper from a stand outside, went in and sat down. The waitress came to take his order.

"Just coffee," he told her.

The stuff she brought him had been cooked down to sludge.

"Black?" she asked.

"It looks that way," he said.

She put a cup of it on the table in front of him and turned away, offended. He had meant to ask her about Loon, but thought better of it. One didn't bring up the subject of insanity in a town like this. One did not push the language to mean more than it did in the dictionary. One did not say, gesturing for a refill of one's coffee cup, "Just half empty, please."

He opened the paper, reading it carefully, interpreting nothing. An Ohio fraternity pledge had choked to death on a calf's liver during initiation hazing. American Nazis prepared to celebrate the birthday of poet Ezra Pound. A woman had murdered her husband with a twelve-pound carp he had caught and thrown in the freezer. Scientists had discovered more holes in the ozone layer. During the previous week, one hundred and fifty lives had been ended by murder squads in Central American countries. Africa had died of thirst. Bangladesh had drowned.

Toward the end of the section containing local news, there was an item noting that Loon, following his arrest for stealing and destroying a trailer house, had once again been remanded to the state mental hospital.

So much for real life, Coyote said to himself. He turned to the comics. When he had finished with them it was getting dark. The waitress, undoubtedly trying to poison him, had been good about refills. He left her all the change in his pockets and walked to his car. He watched how badly the key shook when he put it into the ignition slot. There was a bitter burn in his stomach, a grinding of tooth against tooth in his head. He watched through his windshield as an enormous red moon lifted out of the broken landscape in front of him. Self-induced caffeine psychosis, he thought. He shook his head and drove onto the highway. Once there, he pushed the accelerator to the floor and sped throught the darkening night, obliterating the miles between himself and his home.

A SMALL
GET-TOGETHER

COYOTE WAS IN HIS BACK YARD, lying where the late afternoon sunlight pooled between the shade trees, contemplating a new life as a Zen warrior, when the phone rang. It was the Thoroughbred Mare, wanting him to attend a small get-together at her house that night. He tried to decline.

"No way," he said.

"Don't be stupid," said the Mare. "You've had fun at my parties before."

"I only appeared to have fun. Inside, I suffered."

"Perhaps I should be less delicate," she said. "My husband has left me for someone else. She is younger, far less intelligent, and much more forgiving of his self-centered little mannerisms than I. I need you to be my escort this evening."

"Me?" asked Coyote. "Why me?"

"You are making things difficult. A simple yes or no will do."

"I don't mess around with married ladies."

"You would mess around with rattlesnakes if they were quieter."

"It has to be me?"

"No. It can be any of the jerks who have been hanging around and buying me dinners lately."

"A *grande dame* in distress, eh?"

"You got it."

"What time should I arrive?"

She told him. Coyote sighed as he hung up the phone. Small get-togethers had to be prepared for. Little rituals had to be performed. Zen warriors dealt with their own discordancies before going into battle, knowing the greatest enemies lay within.

He walked out into the yard and found his spot there. He

stretched out prone on the grass, felt the sun on his back, smelled the dank fungusy tang of the earth, unfocused his eyes and saw nothing but sunlit green. Almost immediately, a small black patch began moving about in the greenness and Coyote, startled, pulled back from the lawn and peered at a little black stinkbug making its way through the stalks of grass. The going was not easy. The stinkbug ran headlong into a stalk, climbed up it, and was tipped on its back as it fell down the other side. It struggled for a moment, righted itself, and attacked the next stalk. Coyote picked it up, looked at it briefly, then, overcome by the tiny itchings of stinkbug feet against his skin, threw it several stinkbug miles back in the direction it had come from. Instantly he felt guilty.

A Zen warrior would not have done that, he said to himself. A Zen warrior would have let the stinkbug alone, would have been unbothered by it, would have known that the stinkbug and grass and he, the warrior himself, were part of something greater, something that also included the Zen warrior's enemy, his coming battle, and any cocktail party he might care to go to afterward.

Coyote unfocused his eyes again. He had read that the weight of life beneath the surface of a cow pasture more than equaled the weight of life above it, even when it was full of cows. He saw himself lying not on the grass of his backyard but upon a great squirming layer of bugs and roots and grass, of moles and fungus. He closed his eyes and put his ear to the ground, listening for the earth's heartbeat. Grass spears went into his ear, tickling. He jumped up, shaking his head, feeling a sneeze coming on. Zen warriors probably weren't ticklish, either.

One more try. He knelt, held his head a few inches above the grass, and peered at it intently. He could see each blade of grass. Smaller insects, ones he didn't have names for, scampered beneath the canopy of lawn. He parted grass blades and saw between them the dark wet surface of the dirt, grains of silica glinting in it like tiny eyes. The things he couldn't see, he thought.

Cells in the plants and insects, fragments of humus and clay, bacteria breeding away in schizoid frenzy. Beyond that, endless lattices of molecules, held together by something akin to handshakes. Beyond that, atom families, protons and neutrons in a tight nucleus, orbited by distantly related electrons. Beyond that, nothing, except shadows, brief winds, sly smiles.

From this still perspective, Coyote considered the cocktail party. Find a corner and stay in it, he told himself. Keep your mouth shut. Try not to drink all the gin. Don't sneer at the hors d'oeuvres. Don't call anyone's dress unfortunate. And never throw up on the oriental rug. Simple enough rules. You can remember them.

Thus prepared, Coyote got up from the grass and walked gravely into his house to shower and dress.

When he arrived at the Thoroughbred estate he was wearing grey flannel slacks and a button-down shirt. He was carrying a sheaf of wildflowers he had picked on the way. The Mare opened the door.

"You're on time," she said.

"Surprised?"

"Last time you weren't."

"Last time I wasn't here in an official capacity."

He gave her the flowers, and she took them without comment and put them in a vase on the entry hall table.

"Nobody's here yet. I gave you an hour to get here before everybody else."

"You cut me a lot of slack."

"I was afraid you'd arrive late to get even for being called at the last moment." It was a lie. She smiled and walked to him and ran her fingers down his arm. "You look nice."

"Protective morphology."

She laughed. "I'm sure you'll blend in."

Coyote looked at her, wary, and she laughed again and led him into an enormous room, where great heaps of tiny sandwiches and half-gallon bottles of liquor gave evidence the

Mare's idea of what made up a small get-together was not small. A bartender, hired for the occasion, was busy setting up glasses and napkins and chopping up limes.

The Mare was adjusting some hors d'oeuvres when Coyote felt the usual wave of unreality sweep over him. It happened every time he entered this room. Great beams hung overhead and swept off into the distance toward far walls bright with the works of name-brand artists. A piano the size of an extinct elephant dominated one end of the room. The glass wall it crouched in front of showed a fashionable mountain. The price of a yard of the carpet he was standing on could have bought him a meal at a good restaurant. The bartender and his table were dwarfed by a tapestry that stretched up the wall behind them. As Coyote watched, they continued to shrink in his imagination, getting smaller and smaller until they sank into the weave of the carpet and communed with the things steam cleaners worry about.

One could go into the great cathedrals and get a fair idea of the relative size of God, he thought. Something of the same sort was happening here, the Thoroughbred house having been designed to exalt and glorify a more contemporary deity, the California real estate market. The Mare's husband, the Thoroughbred Stud, had done well there. He had caused this house to be built, paid a decorator to furnish it, had installed his wife in it, housed his children in it, invited his friends over to drink in it, play tennis on its courts, swim in its pool, and be awed by it if they were still of an age and economic status to be capable of awe.

Ah, well. It had apparently been no Nirvana. Much, including the house and kids and the pictures on the walls, would be haggled over in divorce court. The Stud was placing it all in jeopardy for someone, as the Mare described her, young, dumb, and tolerant. Coyote shrugged. There were worse combinations.

He wondered if the Mare had been insufferable, or if the Stud had merely been afflicted with the sort of male mid-life unease that causes one to look upon all of one's works and still find plenty of reason for despair. Certainly the Mare did not look insufferable.

She looked large and athletic and voluptuous and sensual. The faint horsy flavor of her face and bearing might have been a liability had she been smaller, but in her size it called up strong racial memories of fox hunts, high boots, riding crops, clandestine romps in gamekeeper's cottages, and the L.L. Bean catalog. Coyote found her attractive.

He turned to look at her and caught her coming toward him, a tiny sandwich in either hand. She, unlike the bartender, seemed to fit the room.

"What does one do as an escort of the hostess?" he asked, taking one of the sandwiches she offered. It was cut into the shape of a heart. The other sandwiches, he noticed, had been cut into hearts, diamonds, clubs, and spades. One could, he supposed, play solitaire with the food if one failed as an escort.

She smiled. "It's not difficult. You help greet the guests. You tell where the bathroom is. You act comfortable and familiar with the hostess, particularly if her husband is nearby."

"What?"

"Oh, he'll be here. With his little friend. We're being terribly civilized about this separation."

Coyote took a step back from her. "Civilized? What the hell have you gotten me into?"

She reached toward him, ran her hand from his ear to his shoulder, and kissed him gently on the cheek. "Relax," she said. "He's not going to shoot you. People in our socioeconomic class don't do that sort of thing. Besides, he's the one who left me. He'll be paying attention to his friend, who will be telling him how wonderful he is. Of course, you'll have to talk with him."

"I'll what?"

"You'll have to talk with him. It's part of being civilized."

Christ, thought Coyote. These people were supposed to be domesticated. It was amazing how much viciousness could underlie what passed as civilization.

He suddenly relaxed. This was it. The Zen warrior meets the enemy. Two figures on a treeless plain, walking toward each other, faces unmoving, unreadable, almost unrecognizable.

"And what will I have to say?"

"You could say that the weather might turn colder, now that it's getting toward fall. It really doesn't matter what you say, as long as you say something."

"How about if I apologize for being in his house, eating his food, drinking his liquor, and acting comfortable and familiar with his wife?"

She stopped smiling for a moment. "You're taking this much too seriously."

"Probably. I'm just beginning to wonder why you asked me."

He knew why. You did not meet your soon-to-be-ex-husband alone. You were with someone. You appeared to be having a good time. You looked to be taking advantage of your newly bestowed freedom. And if you had a knack for subsurface violence, you were with someone your soon-to-be-ex-husband despised.

Coyote had been on the crew that built the Thoroughbred house. In the early stages of construction, when the hole had been dug for the basement, Coyote and several other workers were down in it, shoveling trenches for the footings of the foundation. It was hot hard work, but it allowed Coyote to put his body on autopilot and think. He had been thinking about the rocks he was exposing to light, wondering how long they had lay buried in darkness, and if they were just dead, inert rocks like they were supposed to be, or if they had souls and thoughts. Were they grateful to be brought out into the air and sunlight? Would they feel regret or horror as the concrete poured over them, locking them in darkness once again?

In the midst of this he heard a voice say, "They're like young, strong animals. They're beautiful."

Another voice said, "They can be anything they want as long as they get my foundation done."

He had looked up and had seen, for the first time, the Thoroughbreds. They were standing on the edge of the hole, contemplating the first of many changes they would make in their original plans for the house. Such changes were to be so extensive and numerous over the course of the construction that when the building contractor died of a burst cerebral aneurysm shortly after finishing the house, Coyote had been sure his death came as a result of redrawing blueprints.

The Mare had been wearing a tennis dress, and from Coyote's vantage point she stood on the horizon, looking like some overheated vision of all that was female. She was long-legged and dark-maned and blindingly white and heroically curved against a dark blue sky.

During the lunch break, while the Stud was walking around the property with the contractor, Coyote walked up to the Mare.

"Hi," he said. "I'm a young strong animal. Can you get loose for an evening?"

She reddened. "You weren't supposed to hear that."

"Then you weren't supposed to talk so loud."

"You're building our house," she said brightly and loudly. "Mine and my husband's and my children's."

"Are you happily married?" Coyote was feeling the faint beginnings of an urge to be rude.

She ignored the question. "How do you like your work?" she asked, still in the same bright tone, but looking around nervously for her husband.

The urge to rudeness almost went away. "It's inspiring," said Coyote. He pointed into the pit. "In a little while there will be a concrete foundation down there. You can see your life in that sort of thing. Like tea leaves."

"Your life?"

"Sure. First you dig a hole and set up the forms. That's all preparation, similar to starting a career or getting married or being born to wealth. Then you fill the forms with wet concrete. That's like the raw stuff of your existence, the pure energy you

31

pour into what you're doing, the streams of movement and thought that explore your boundaries and limits. Then there's a period of waiting, a gradual settling in, a getting used to things. Then they take the forms away and there you are, stuck in a hole, rigid, unable to move an inch, ever."

She looked at him closely, a little amused, no longer nervous. "For a young, strong, beautiful animal, you're awfully depressing."

He shrugged. "I'm not sure it always works that way."

She studied him, all traces of amusement gone from her face. "Really? How very fortunate for you to be able to think so."

The Stud had returned, motioning for the Mare to follow him to their car. She waved him away. "I'm talking to one of the workers," she said. "He's a sort of philosopher."

"I'm not paying for philosophy," said the Stud. "I'm paying for concrete. Come on."

She had given him a smile and left. Coyote watched the swaying of her hips all the way to the car, had shrugged mournfully, and had gone back to his shovel and rocks.

At their housewarming party, to which he had been invited, Coyote had indeed tried to drink all the gin and had indeed thrown up on the oriental rug. At the party following that he had made tasteless jokes about the dwarves who had made the hors d'oeuvres and at the one after that he had suggested that someone's designer gown bore a striking resemblance to the oriental rug after he had thrown up on it. At the one after that, the Stud, apparently oblivious to all that had gone before, mistook him for a real guest and tried to make conversation with him.

"What do you think of the house?" asked the Stud.

"It's got a good foundation."

"It cost me twice what it's worth, but I'll sell it for twice what I paid."

"That's good," said Coyote.

"We've been coming here for years. Vacations. I've finally

fixed it so I can do most of my business by phone. If you've got a computer and a fax machine you can live anywhere."

Coyote began looking around the room, feeling the first flickerings of cocktail party claustrophobia. He turned back to the Stud, showing a bit too much of the whites of his eyes.

"You can do anything over a phone line now," said the Stud. "Take me. I've just put in an office in this house. I run the business out of my bedroom. I can buy and sell every bit as well in my pajamas as I can in a three-piece suit. Maybe better."

Coyote suppressed a shudder. No one, least of all the Mare, appeared to be about to rescue him. What the hell, he thought. "What is it you buy and sell?" he asked.

"Things," said the Stud. "Usually I buy them for less than I sell them for."

"That's the best way," said Coyote.

The Stud nodded. "The trouble with most people, they're not quick enough. Something goes up in value and they don't realize it. Take a piece of land, for instance. People think it's going to go up in value. If they even think that, it's already gone up in value."

The Stud paused significantly. Coyote gave him a solemn nod.

"What you're trying to tell me is that you're a speculator."

The Stud frowned. "There are good, tax-free reasons for not using that word in my business. Let's just say I make a comfortable living by positioning myself between someone who wants something very badly and the person who owns whatever that something is." He looked sharply at Coyote. "What is it you do, anyway?"

"I helped build your house," said Coyote. "We've met before."

The Stud's face lost all expression. "Oh," he said. "You're the one." Then he turned and walked off.

It had been the Mare who had kept inviting Coyote to the parties even when the number of people he had offended reached triple figures. And even on the days after, when he cringed at the memory of what he had said and done, he was grateful to her for the opportunity to have seen her and talked with her, however briefly. Over the course of a dozen parties, they had become friends. Several times, drunk, he had invited her to run away with him to far away romantic places—usually clumps of shrubbery within walking distance—but each time she had smiled indulgently at him and said she preferred her own turf. Once she had told him her marriage was a lonely one. He had not asked for details, having been content with what his eyes had seen and his ears had heard. It was indeed a lonely marriage, he judged, marked by unhappy yearnings for young strong animals of both sexes.

All this passed through the mind of the would-be Zen warrior Coyote as he waited for the Mare to tell him why she had asked him to her house.

She had given him a cool stare for a long moment, finally saying, "I asked you because I like you. No other reason."

Coyote was trying to find reason to believe her when a car drove into the driveway. It was the Stud, alone. He got out and a few moments later they heard him in the entry hall.

"Wait here," said the Mare. She left the room and pulled the door behind her.

"Where'd you get the weeds?" asked the Stud. The door slammed shut, making her reply mercifully indistinct.

Coyote drifted over to the bartender's table and was handed a tall gin-and–tonic. He nodded his thanks and walked to the piano, resting his elbows on its lower jaw and contemplating its innards.

From the sounds of the voices, they were negotiating out there. The Stud's tone, initially scornful, was beginning to sound hurt and angry. The Mare, at first hurt and angry, was beginning to sound triumphant.

Something must have gone wrong with the young dumb agreeable one. Maybe the Stud had changed his mind. Maybe he had studied the vagaries of the stock and real estate markets and had concluded he couldn't do it all over again. Maybe he had talked to his lawyer and had been told a divorce would be an economic disaster. Maybe he had decided he still loved her. Maybe Coyote himself had been a hole card in a game between them, a game played hard and for keeps.

What was a Zen warrior to do? Coyote turned to look out the window and as he did, his tall glass, beaded with dewdrops, slipped from his fingers and fell into the piano. There was a great gong as the glass hit piano wire, and the sound of gin-and-tonic sloshing down into the recesses of the instrument. He looked around. The bartender, unless he was completely deaf, was ignoring both the sounds in the hallway and the still-reverberating piano. They ought to equip these things with bilge pumps, thought Coyote, looking down into a metallic gin-and-tonic reflection of himself.

Shouting began in the hallway. Coyote picked up his empty glass and stared into it. A Zen warrior should know when not to fight, he thought. A Zen warrior should know when he's up against something that cannot fit in his universe. A Zen warrior should know when it is that even when he's made allies of all the enemies within, he's still going to get his ass kicked.

This was one of those times. Coyote stepped to an open bay window and reached through it and lifted a screen out of its frame. He dropped the screen on the ground outside and stepped through into an exquisitely manicured flower garden. He picked his way through the flowers to the hedge separating the garden from the driveway in time to peek over it and see the Stud, his eyes blindered by rage and despair, climb into his car and roar away, leaving behind only a great cloud of tiresmoke and the echoes of a redlined engine.

The trick is to forgive, thought Coyote. You have to see everything very clearly and honestly and still let it go. You are in this world but not of it. Remember that. It's easier on drive-line components.

Do Zen warriors take their own advice? Coyote looked back across the garden to the open window. Through it, he could see the piano, and beyond the piano the Mare. She was talking to the bartender, who was pointing out into the garden. I should run now, thought Coyote. I should run now and forgive myself later.

But he didn't. He was still standing on the edge of the garden when the Mare came to the window and saw him. She asked him what he was doing. He told her he didn't know. She called him back to her, and he went. She helped him through the window and into the great room. Then she took his arm, and together—having forgiven each other for the moment—the Mare and the warrior went to greet the arriving guests.

OBJECT LESSONS

COYOTE, OUT WALKING THE TOWN in the early morning, watched as dead leaves fell from trees, spiraled down through still air, and lay unmoving in his path. Around him, the dark houses, the silent streets and parked cars, and the dry hills that rose above the rooftops all looked unhealthily pastel beneath a coating of frost and shadow.

He had gotten up that morning overwhelmed by the need to read the newspaper and eat breakfast in a warm restaurant. Powerful Coyote hormones were agitating for a place where waitresses were competent and cheerful and moved with unconscious feminine grace. There had been no possibility of doing what he usually did, which was to turn off the alarm and dive back under a down comforter.

He walked into a cafe that had big windows and decent coffee, bought a paper from the machine by the cash register and sat down at a table. His friend Otter was waiting tables and came to take his order.

"What are you doing up so early?" she asked.

Coyote relaxed in the warmth of the room, smelled hot coffee and frying bacon, and looked approvingly at Otter, who appeared sleek and streamlined in her black rayon uniform. He noted she moved with easy—but not unconscious—feminine grace.

"Following basic urges," he said.

She smiled. "That's the nicest thing anybody's said to me all day."

He ordered breakfast. She went to the kitchen and came back with two cups of coffee, gave him one and sat down across the table from him. It was still early and there were only a few customers.

"So how's your life?" asked Coyote.

Otter's smile began slowly. It ended showing lots of teeth.

"You're not going to believe this one," she said. She waited a moment, then said, "You know him."

"I've known most of them," said Coyote.

In the years since her divorce, Otter had made up for the lost and unlucky thirteen years of her marriage. At an age usually given over to worries about settling down and biological clocks, Otter had begun to worry about romance. She had begun a string of affairs, all of them marked by candlelit dinners and surprise bouquets, essential nutrients her marriage had lacked.

"That's how you can tell if it's the real thing," she had told Coyote. "They buy you dinner in places that aren't tacky. They buy you flowers. And they look at you but they do not see you."

"What happens when the flowers die and the dinners start coming from the microwave and they begin wearing glasses again?" Coyote had asked.

"That's when it's not the real thing anymore," she had said.

"So are you going to guess who it is?" Otter was looking at Coyote impatiently.

Coyote shook his head. "Surprise me."

"Your friend Sandhill."

"Sandhill? Sandhill Crane?" Coyote turned a little away from her and looked at her out of the corners of his eyes. Sandhill Crane was an upright member of the community, a school teacher with a wife and family.

"He loves me," Otter said.

"He can't love you," said Coyote. "He has kids. He reads to them out of Little Golden Books. And they adopted that little baby whooper just last year. His wife mends his clothes and cans the garden every year and organizes anti-nuclear fund drives. How could you do such a thing?"

Otter smiled out at him from a moral Eden. "Don't you know what it's like to be in love?"

"I haven't had as much practice as some people."

She ignored him. "He brings me roses. Single, long-stemmed roses. He comes in to see me every morning before school."

"You homewrecker."

Otter stood up and looked around the room. "He says he'll take me away from all this. He knows about a place in the Alaskan mountains. A little valley with a stream running down the middle of it. He's going to build me a log cabin."

"And you'll grow your own food?"

She nodded.

"And make your own clothes out of skins and stuff?"

"He calls it getting out of the consumer economy."

"Then he'd better stick with his wife. She's been making do without the consumer economy for years. You have to, on a teacher's salary."

Otter finally got angry. "People get to dream a little, don't they? Besides, there are a few things I'm better at than his wife." She walked toward the kitchen. "Since when did you become a protector of marriages and children, anyway?"

Coyote sighed and stared at the steam curling out of his coffee into the horizon-weakened sunlight. Spring, not fall, was supposed to be the season when this sort of thing happened. Not that it made any difference with Otter. She seemed to carry an eternally recurring springtime within herself. By placing his ear close to her heart, he supposed, he would be able to hear the sounds of birds fluttering, bees buzzing, and tiny meadow flowers whispering in a warm breeze. It was not easy to condemn such a thing, even when it goaded a solid and predictable husband into a desperate awareness of his capacity for love.

For her part, Otter threw herself into each new affair with the fervor of a true believer. She accepted the flowers and dinners as sacramental symbols, shining lights that banished a dark world of silent home-cooked dinners, lump-filled reclining chairs in front of flickering TV sets, sad afternoon bathrobes, IRA's, lawns that wouldn't stay mowed, cars that wouldn't stay fixed. It was only when a moment of conscience intruded on the ritual—a child's birthday perhaps, or a wife's resigned forgiveness—that Otter would abruptly throw the poor guy out of her life and wait for someone else to come up with the proper floral preliminaries.

He looked out the window. There had been times when he considered buying her a rose or two himself, but had thought better of it. It would be a little like getting into a barrel just above Niagara Falls, he had decided. Life would be beyond control from when you got in until you were bouncing around amid the rocks and foam at the bottom, suffering from multiple internal injuries and wondering how you ever could have thought you were going to get away with it.

Sandhill Crane's car turned quickly into the parking lot and rocked to a stop. Sandhill got out, slammed the car door, and began walking toward the restaurant. He stopped, went to the car again, reached in and retrieved his briefcase. A triangle of translucent green florist's paper was sticking from between its hinges.

Sandhill hurried across the parking lot, twisting his long neck to glance nervously around town, looking like an unimaginative and trustworthy accountant heading off to Rio with his company payroll. He came through the door and stood gazing around through warmth-fogged glasses. He managed to spot Coyote, waved, walked over, and sat down.

"I hate this time of year," he said, pulling off the glasses and wiping them with a paper napkin. "It's freezing. The leaves all die. Suddenly I realize I'm a year older. I get stuck behind the school bus on the way to work. My students look out the back windows and point and make faces."

"You told me the same thing last year," said Coyote.

"I suppose I did. The same thing happened last year."

"You shouldn't let it bother you."

"I shouldn't let it bother me," Sandhill mimicked. "Just like the frost on my windshield that takes ten minutes to scrape off and makes me late for work. I can't do anything about it, so I shouldn't let it bother me. It gets cold. Frost forms. I'm late. I get older. Students make faces. It bothers me. Okay?"

Otter came out of the kitchen. Sandhill jumped up as she approached their table. He reached into his briefcase, pulled out a rose, and shook it to fluff it up a bit. He then picked up a small vase filled with straw flowers off the windowsill. He held the vase by its bottom and flung the flowers out onto the floor in a wide semicircle. Then he stuck the rose in the vase and handed it to Otter.

"My love," he said.

Otter looked at Sandhill, then at the rose, and then at the flowers scattered about.

"You're so romantic," she said to Sandhill. "Isn't he?" she asked Coyote.

"Who's going to clean up the floor?" Coyote asked.

"Don't be disgusting," she said. She turned again to Sandhill, kissed him on the cheek and went off to the kitchen to put water in the vase and to pour in the little packet of flower preserver that was stapled to the rose stem. Sandhill got down on his knees and began picking up straw flowers. When he was done he put them all in the ashtray on Coyote's table and sat down again.

"I suppose you think I'm nuts," he said.

"Oh, no," said Coyote.

"I can tell what you're thinking. You're wondering how I could do this to my wife and kids. How I can be a role model for my students if I'm sneaking around, having a cheap little affair."

Coyote looked at his unread paper with regret. "I wasn't wondering anything like that." What he had been wondering was how Otter got out of these things once she got into them.

"How old do you think I am?" Sandhill demanded.

"I don't know."

"I'm lost in the forties," said Sandhill. "Lost in the forties. That's how old I am." He paused.

"It's hard being a teacher," he said. "You start every year and they all come into your classes with bright faces and new running shoes and enthusiasm and trust that you know what you're talking about. And if you live up to that trust, if you do your job and teach them to really wonder about the world and really look at it instead of seeing what they've always been told to see, then they begin to learn without you. And then they turn into these wonderful creatures who graduate and go off and lead real lives. They do things. And then you start over."

"That doesn't sound so bad," said Coyote. "You're helping them, anyway."

"I don't want to help them. I want to be alive. I want to go with them." Sandhill gave him a bleak stare. "New designer colors," he muttered.

"What?"

"New designer colors on their running shoes. That's what changes in your life. And all the time you're getting older. The years go by in bundles of twenty."

"For everybody," said Coyote. "Even for people with real lives."

"Everybody keeps growing up," said Sandhill. "Even my kids are growing up."

"What do you want? Dwarves?"

"You don't understand. People you care about grow up. You lose them. They go away. They disappear. I used to love a girl who became my wife. She's gone. She's been replaced by some strange woman who looks at me and sees only my bad knee and my bald head and my paycheck, and who reminds me that my dental checkup is due so I can fight a losing battle with tooth decay. How can you love someone when they keep reminding you your teeth are rotting?"

"Love," said Coyote, eyeing the kitchen.

"Oh, no," said Sandhill. "It's not that easy a diagnosis. I know what I'm doing. I have no illusions about this. If she wants to play at love, I'll play at love. If that's the price for doing what I'm doing, I'll pay it. This is no typical midlife crisis."

God help you, thought Coyote. Even if it is.

"She's going away with me, you know," said Sandhill as he gestured toward the kitchen. "Maybe it's because she loves me. Maybe she just wants to break out of her life like I do." He lowered his voice to a near-whisper. "I took all the money out of my teacher's retirement fund. Bought a four–wheel-drive pickup. It's in a friend's garage."

"How are you going to live? What are you going to do?"

"Aha," said Sandhill. "I've thought that out, too. We're putting the pickup on a ship and sailing up the inland passage to Alaska."

Coyote nodded.

"Alaska," Sandhill repeated, and Coyote thought it made a beautiful sound when he said it.

"It's fall," said Coyote. "It's dark in Alaska."

"I'll get a job teaching in the bush," said Sandhill. "One of my former students is a school administrator up there."

"Aren't you afraid your students will still grow up and leave you?"

"Not if he's my boss." Sandhill shook his head, irritated. "I didn't come in here to explain this to you. I've got to leave for school soon, and you're missing my point entirely." He reached into his pocket and pulled out a cigarette lighter. "But I'll demonstrate."

He flicked the lighter and touched its flame to the dried flowers in the ashtray. They bloomed into a quick fire that rose a foot and then died, and a tiny mushroom cloud of smoke began rising toward the ceiling. There was a sharp pop as the ashtray cracked. Some of the flowers, miraculously keeping their form, glowed against the blackened glass.

"That's what happens to you," said Sandhill. "You burn out."

Sandhill had done too many classroom demonstrations, had made too many trips to the audiovisual room. The occupation was full of hazards, and acquiring the need to give object lessons was apparently one of them. Coyote poured an inch of cold coffee from his cup into the ashtray and stopped the smoke.

"We'll send you a postcard," said Sandhill. He stood and picked up his briefcase in a single strong motion. He intercepted Otter on her way back to the kitchen from a table. He followed her through the swinging kitchen door, and through its small window Coyote watched him kiss her full on the lips and look deep into her eyes. Coyote turned away with a little shudder. Speaking of occupational hazards, he thought. Most voyeurs probably end up cynics.

Sandhill came out of the kitchen and strode to the door.

"Don't get caught," said Coyote, "behind a school bus."

There was no reply. Sandhill hurried out and ran across the parking lot to his car. His briefcase banged against his legs. He opened his car door, threw his briefcase across the seat, looked at his watch, jumped in and slammed the door on his coat, opened it, pulled his coat in, and slammed it again. There was a period of about thirty seconds when the old car refused to start, but it finally did and Sandhill pulled into the morning traffic and was gone.

Otter came out of the kitchen with his breakfast and a new pot of coffee.

"Your friend's in a hurry," said Coyote.

"He's always in a hurry," she said. "He can't wait for the semester to be over. He counts the days."

Coyote considered Sandhill's brief summers, when he must have done everything he could to slow down the minutes, must have walked out in the sun each hour, telling himself, "Right now I am feeling hot light on my back and the wind and blue sky and wet green grass and the world solid under my feet." And then the inevitable waiting until next year once the calendar began to fold and the days began an accelerating slide into the loss column. No wonder Sandhill had fallen for Otter's peculiar brand of seduction. "When are you leaving for Alaska?" said Coyote.

Otter sighed. "No," she said. She gave him a tragic look. "I'm not going."

"No?"

"It would be hard to stay in love all night long up there. Even for me."

"You could really get to know each other," said Coyote.

"That doesn't always help you stay in love," said Otter. "I'll take my chances down here, where there are nice restaurants and lots of nice people to take you to them."

"Who it is that takes you doesn't matter?"

"A little. But it doesn't matter as much as the feeling of those first few times you go out with someone." She smiled, remembering something delicious. "Starting something new is the best feeling in the world."

"What about ending something old?"

"That doesn't feel so good," said Otter. "But I always surprise myself. I can have these incredibly deep, close feelings one day and the next day they're gone. I always think it's going to hurt, but it doesn't."

What Otter lacked in staying power, thought Coyote, she made up for in honesty.

"Don't you ever just want to be alone?" Fewer people might get hurt, he thought, if Otter spent more time alone.

"I am alone," said Otter. "Aren't you?" She left him there with two eggs and several pieces of toast and a sausage patty.

I should have gone to a restaurant where I didn't know anybody, thought Coyote. He stared out the window and across town to the forested northern slopes of the hills. Wood gathering time. Time to go out on the mountain roads and look for trees that are good and dead, chainsaw them into pieces and throw them into the back of a pickup, take them home and offer them to the friendly and warm little god who lives in the woodstove all winter.

He felt better thinking about this. He resolved to do a better job borrowing a pickup this year than he had last, when the woodpile he had scraped together during the final few days before the snow fell had lasted only into the first real cold spell of the winter. With his woodpile gone, he had been reduced to feeding his landlord's furnishings—an old sideboard and three or four chairs—into the stove one chill, grey day. Then at dark he had grabbed a neighbor kid's saucer sled and had made twenty-five or thirty trips to the wood supply of a nearby condominium complex and had gotten enough wood to last until April. The first few trips had been fine but after that he had become lonely and scared and had started feeling sorry for himself.

Coyote grinned. Sandhill had a pickup, waxed and polished and ready, sitting in an anonymous garage. It was perfectly suited to woodgathering— had probably been designed with woodgathering in mind. He would have to tell Sandhill what an adventure wandering through the woods with a chainsaw could be.

He finished eating and stood by the cash register at the door waiting for Otter to come with his check. He paid her and started to go.

"What are you up to today?" she asked.

"Woodcutting," he said. He turned away, then turned back and said, "How old are you?"

She watched him warily. "I'll be thirty-eight next spring." When she saw the expression on his face she said, "But don't let it bother you. I'll find someone sometime, before it's too late."

"Does it get too late?" he asked.

She shook her head. "I don't think so. But if it does, I'll do fine. You don't need to worry about me."

"I won't," said Coyote, turning away again and heading for the door. "I really won't."

USER FRIENDLY

AT THE COLD LIGHT OF DAY Coyote climbed out of bed, noted the drifts of snow at the bottom of his windowpanes, and ran across the frozen floor of his house. He pulled two logs from the woodbox and threw them on the fading coals in his stove. He opened the damper, turned, ran back to his bed, jumped in and pulled the covers up over his nose. He waited for the muffled explosion of logs catching flame. Life can be worse, he told himself, than when you're in a warm bed in a cold room where the stove has just taken off.

It was still snowing, to judge from the sounds that came from outside. The noises of a normal day—shouts of children going to school, cars in the street, doors slamming, dogs barking—all were soft and indistinct. Coyote closed his eyes. Maybe he would stay in bed all day. He had plenty of books and plenty of pillows, and he could live on cocoa and cereal until dark. Then he could go out and find a bar that would serve him a hamburger with his beer. He could watch the news on its television and find out what had happened in the world while he had been away from it. It was a plan. He relaxed and fell toward a dark ocean of sleep.

Something stopped him. Some memory floating on the surface of dream, something he was supposed to do today. An obligation to a friend.

Friend? Most of Coyote's friendships carried no obligations, only an unexpressed requirement for shared perceptions. Someone who saw things the way he did was a far truer friend to him than someone he could borrow a snow shovel from. And what could he owe a friend of that sort? A point, a nod, a wink. That was all.

Wait. Coyote opened his eyes. He remembered.

Loon was being let out today. Loon had been declared cured, sane, no longer the menace to life and property he had once been. He was arriving today by bus, and was to stay with Coyote while he looked for a job and a place to live. Coyote sighed, feeling the grim arrival of a promise made when its fulfillment had seemed safe in the improbable future.

He had gone to visit Loon. He had driven through the gates of the state mental hospital and had walked into the waiting room. A young doctor who introduced himself as Owl waited there to escort him deeper into the building.

"Your friend is an interesting case," said Owl, as he unlocked a glass door. A grid of shiny wire was imbedded in it.

"Dangerous?"

"Oh, no," said Owl, unlocking another door. It was made of heavy wood and had no window at all. "But it's doubtful you'll be able to get through to him. He's assumed several identities since he's come here. Each time he's depersonalized a little more."

They went down a flight of stairs and Coyote realized, with a sudden look at the steps up over his shoulder, that he had assumed Loon's prison would be above ground, where light and air could penetrate. Owl unlocked a third door, one of grey steel, with no sign or marking on it to indicate what lay on the other side.

"Your friend thinks he's a computer," said Owl. They went in, and there in the thick fouled atmosphere of a high-security mental ward, in the dim light of window wells, they found Loon.

He was perched on the edge of a bed that was bolted to the floor. He did not move when they approached him. Coyote pulled up a chair, sat down and put his face in line with Loon's gaze. There was no instant of recognition in Loon's eyes, no indication he had ever known Coyote. Loon was simply not there—if there was something that remained of the person he had been, it was hidden, driven into some dark interior corner, away from the windows of his eyes.

"Does he see me?" Coyote asked. Fear was welling up inside of him. This Loon was not Loon. It was not anyone he knew. Coyote felt the solid ground of memory shift. Had he ever been a friend in those eyes he sat in front of?

"We don't know what he sees," said Owl. "There's only one way to get him to respond to anything." He reached behind Loon's ear and made a flicking motion. Loon began making a humming noise. His jaw dropped. Owl reached into his white coat and pulled out a cracker. He put it in Loon's mouth. Loon slowly chewed and swallowed it.

"Unauthorized replication of this software is expressly prohibited by law," said Loon, blowing crumbs. "Violators will be prosecuted, and they *will become a terror to themselves and their friends; they will be delivered into the hands of their enemies; their eyes will be plucked out and they will live in darkness forever; and they will be broken as a vessel smashed upon the ground and will not be made whole again.*"

"That seems to be the message on every cracker he eats," said Owl.

"I'll bet nobody is sneaking in pirated copies of crackers from Taiwan," said Coyote.

"He's lifted that from the Old Testament," said Owl. "Right after he came here, he thought he was a TV evangelist. That personality still shows up on his software."

"File name?" Loon asked abruptly.

"Why don't we go over what we covered last time?" suggested Owl.

Loon emitted a series of beeps and clicks. "I suppose," he said mechanically, "that one could take on the persona of a computer to escape the pain of living in an imperfect and tragic world. A computer cannot feel. It cannot empathize. Prick it, and it does not bleed. Insult it, and it does not feel anger. Accuse it, and it feels no guilt. All the terror and agony we are heir to are of no importance to it. It remembers facts, only facts, and the fact of a child's death and the fact of a lily opening to the sun are, to it, equal in value."

"That's what I said to him a week ago, word for word," said Owl. He looked sheepish. "I get a little poetic around catatonics. As if my eloquence could make up for their emptiness and silence."

"I am reminded," said Loon, "of studies done in the early 1950's on schizophrenic children. Given crayons and paper, these children would draw pictures of themselves remarkably similar to those drawn by children who were not disturbed. With one important exception. These crayoned self‑images had electrical cords growing out of them, symbolic umbilici to the fabulous post-war world of chromed toasters, electric can openers, hundred‑pound television sets that gazed unseeing with great blue eyes. Turn these things on and they worked perfectly at simple tasks. Turn them off and they were—off. Becoming an electrical appliance was an answer to the conundrum of being."

"I said that, too," said Owl.

"I recognized your style," said Coyote.

Loon again began making pops and clicks. "Anniversary the fifteenth. Don't forget to order flowers. Birthday the twenty-third. Susie. Barbie Doll? Thirty-thousand mile service on car. Make appointment today."

"Was that you, too?" Coyote asked.

Owl coughed. "I always forget things. He doesn't."

Seeing Coyote's horrified look, Owl said, "We try to give our patients occupational therapy. What am I going to have him doing? Basket weaving? Computers don't weave baskets."

An older doctor came into the room and gazed at the still figure on the bed.

"Still pushing your computer metaphor, eh, Owl?"

Owl turned. "Dr. Coot," he said.

"You young doctors think you have to set the world on fire," said Coot. "This new theory, that new theory." Loon's jaw had dropped open again. "Look at that slack-jawed, anesthetized look," said Coot. "That listless gaze. For all we know, he thinks he's watching the Carson monologue."

"He thinks he's a computer," said Owl.

"In my professional judgement, you're wrong," said Coot. "He's simply an extreme case of what is happening out there, beyond these walls. They're locked on to their televisions, staring at themselves in barroom mirrors, smoking dope and gazing without comprehension at a world dreamed up by third-rate entertainers and fourth-rate architects. It's the widespread death of consciousness that's been prophesied in the literature since Freud. *Eruptus dementiae adenoidae.* The scourge of the mouthbreathers. What's this?" Coot had turned to Coyote. "Another one?"

Coyote had been listening to him, mouth agape. He closed it quickly.

Coot looked him over with a practiced eye. "The usual personality disorders and antisocial tendencies. Simple paranoid fantasies in conjunction with a childish narcissism. A socialized schizophrenia allowing near-perfect separation of the different arenas of his life. You're not sick," he said. He turned back to Owl. "Release this patient at once."

"He's not a patient," said Owl.

"Oh," said Coot. "Well, I could have told you that." He turned away and stalked out of the ward.

"Was that your boss?" Coyote asked.

"Hardly," said Owl, offended. "He's been a patient here for years."

"You let him pretend he's a psychiatrist?"

"Actually, he's been involved in a number of amazing cures. He's reached some of the ones everyone else had given up on."

"You better let him work with this one," Coyote said, pointing at Loon.

"We seem to be coming along quite well without his help," Owl murmured. He reached in his pocket and got another cracker. He put it in Loon's open mouth. Loon spat it out.

"*Disk full error,*" said Loon.

"He always says that when he's had enough crackers," said Owl. "He won't respond anymore until he gets hungry."

"Get me out of here," said Coyote. Soft green institutional walls, their surfaces rounded by pale shadow, were beginning to close in.

Owl smiled and reached for his keys. "Simple claustrophobia is a normal reaction," he said." It's nothing to be worried about."

Loon still had not moved. "GET ME OUT OF HERE," yelled Coyote.

"Okay, okay," said Owl. "You were the one who wanted to see him."

Owl methodically led him up through the three doors, opening and locking them again with care, pretending to ignore Coyote's panic. When Coyote reached the waiting room he ran out of it and down the front steps and across the grounds to his car.

It had been a long and sad drive home. When he got back to his house, Coyote looked at several of the large, ink-blot-like paintings Loon had done that were on his walls, scanning them for hints of dissolution, craziness, cracks in their surfaces through which he could see the simple bed that Loon now occupied. But nothing was there. Or rather, everything was there. Mad shapes were whirling within all of them. A splotch of brown became a sick bat. Soft reds turned to blood. Tiny bits of day-glo green became piggy little staring eyes. But it was Coyote who saw these things. They had not been there when Loon had layered paint on the canvasses. Coyote considered the implications of this, took down the paintings and stored them in a closet.

Then, a month ago, there had come a phone call.

"I'm getting out," Loon had said. "I've got a certificate that says I'm sane."

That's more than I've got, thought Coyote. Loon went on to

ask him if he could stay with him for awhile. "They like for us to have a place to go to," said Loon. "Dr. Coot recommended I contact you."

In the end Coyote had told Loon to stay as long as he wanted and had offered to help him find a job. Dishwashing jobs were plentiful as soon as the skiers started coming to town. If enough snow came, there would be roof-shoveling to do. Coyote wasn't sure what Loon could handle, but decided that shoveling a roof slowly and deliberately, carefully cutting snow into large blocks and easing them off the edge of a roof might be the sort of concrete activity that would be good for someone in Loon's recently sane condition.

And finally the day had come. Coyote had to go down to the bus station and pick Loon up and hope that Loon wasn't so fragile he would break on the way back home.

Coyote got out of bed, hurried over to the stove with his clothes, and dressed. He pulled on boots and went out to warm up his car. The snow surprised and cheered him. Snow is good for the spirit, he thought. It puts a smooth blanket on unraked lawns. It covers up beer cans in gutters. It makes light lighter. Underneath a foot of snow, my car could be new.

It was only a temporary cover, he knew. Brief insulation from detail. It would melt, and ugly things would lie exposed once again. But by then it would be spring. In the meantime he was happy that a bare tree, all grey claws and dry screams the day before it snowed, could be a forty-foot pom- pom the day after.

He brushed the snow from his car, started it, and went back in while it warmed up. He put out a folding cot for Loon, piled blankets and bedding on it, and picked up books and papers off the floor. He started to take one of Loon's paintings from the closet, thought better of it, and put it back. Loon had probably seen enough ink blots to last him awhile.

Coyote went out to his car and began driving to the station. On the way he made a disturbing connection between Loon's insanity and the way the snow turned the dreary objects of fall into the beautiful abstracts of winter. Loon mad had retained only the words of others as his reality, had dealt in symbols without meaning. Had he enjoyed the pure sounds of the words he spoke as much as Coyote enjoyed the pure shapes of a town covered by snow? Coyote had no way of knowing. What he was sure of was that even the psychiatrists Coot and Owl, sane or not, found they had to weave a safety net of words between themselves and the reality of Loon's blind stare.

When the bus pulled into the station Loon wasn't on it. Coyote waited until the last passenger had stepped off, then asked the bus driver if he had seen Loon. No one of that description had gotten on the bus. Ah, Loon, thought Coyote. You're sitting alone again, and still, on some bench in some far station. People come and go and pay no attention to you. The ticket seller thinks you're asleep.

He was deciding whom to call when a car pulled up behind him and stopped. Loon got out of the driver's seat, walked up to him and said, "It's good to see you, friend."

"Loon?" asked Coyote.

"Who else?" asked Loon.

Loon looked good. He spoke as Coyote remembered Loon speaking. He moved as Coyote remembered Loon moving.

"I won't be staying with you," said Loon. "I've been out a week already. I have a job and an apartment in town. Anyway, thanks for coming to pick me up. Let me buy you breakfast."

"Are you all right?" asked Coyote. "The last time I saw you, you thought you were a computer."

"I am a computer," said Loon. "Get in the car."

Because he didn't know what else to do, and because Loon had already gotten back behind the wheel, Coyote opened the passenger door and got in. He sank into soft leather.

"Like the car?" asked Loon as they drove away. "My company leases it for me. It's one of the perks of the position. Besides, you can't sell real estate riding around on shoddy wheels."

"I like it," said Coyote. "What do you mean you're still a computer?"

"It's what I've always been," said Loon. "It's just that I've incorporated a number of recent advances in the field. Parallel processing, holographic storage, self-programming capabilities." He tapped the side of his skull. "I've got gigabytes in here. Gigabytes."

"But you don't sound like a computer."

"What's one sound like? Like last year's voice synthesizer, right? Listen. This field is moving very fast. A personality can be put into digital form as easily as a Pac-man game. Interface a personality program with a hard-wired positive attitude and all you have to do is pick up the appropriate occupational software. I was able to download my files from a manic-depressive real-estate salesman. Two days after I got out I was working for his old firm. Yesterday I sold my first house."

"You've got a job," said Coyote, in disbelief.

"A good one. Great people to work with. Great people to deal with. And listen, friend, it takes only a few well-programmed kilobytes to get rich in this market. Somebody wants to sell, somebody wants to buy. All you do is get them together."

"Loon, is everything all right with you?" asked Coyote.

Loon looked puzzled. "All systems and programs are functioning without glitches," he said.

"What are you doing with your art? What are you painting these days?"

Loon looked at him, uncomprehending. "Retrieve on stated index failed," he said.

"Huh?" asked Coyote.

"Retrieve on stated index failed."

"That's what I thought you said," said Coyote.

Loon smiled. "I can whip up some dandy multicolored pie graphs if that's what you want."

"What do you do for fun?"

"That's easy. Raquetball. I also swim. Ski. My brokerage has a membership in a local health club. I work out on the weight machines." Loon grinned. "Some of the female members have very advanced mainframes."

Loon stopped the car in front of a restaurant Coyote had avoided because the menu posted outside didn't have any prices on it. The place was packed. "Have you eaten here?" Loon asked. "My clients say it has a great brunch."

Coyote shook his head. Loon got out of the car, closed his door and locked it. Coyote sat still. "Lock your door," said Loon. "I just had a digital sound system installed."

Coyote didn't move. He looked at Loon, but instead of thinking of Loon he thought of all those others, the ones he had known who had become lawyers and accountants and teachers and advertising executives. They had willingly strapped themselves into a great economic Nautilus machine and they were exercising like crazy right now. They had car weights on their hands, house weights on their feet, and they struggled and sweated and matched their moves to that of the machine until it was hard to tell where the machine stopped and the person started. Now he was about to have brunch with a whole bunch of them.

"Don't just sit there," said Loon. "We've got to get a table."

And they wouldn't think anything was wrong with Loon, thought Coyote. They'd talk stocks with him in the jacuzzi of the health club, discuss car performance with him on the chairlift, invite him to wine tastings, compare stereos and vacations. Loon's software could handle it.

"What are you waiting for?" said Loon.

It was still snowing. Large feathery flakes were beginning to stick to the windshield, making it hard to see Loon, who was looking in at Coyote. Something was wrong with Loon's eyes.

"What's the matter with you?" Loon screamed through the glass. "Aren't you hungry?"

Coyote watched the snow hit the windshield and magically stop. Soon it would cover the car like a soft cocoon. He could stay where he was, burrow into the fresh leather, listen to the stereo, and no one would know he was there.

Loon jerked open the passenger door. "You going to sit there all day?"

"Take it easy," said Coyote. "I was just thinking."

He got out then, and went in and ate with his friend Loon. But it was not Loon, and not his friend, and although the crab in the omelette had been flown in fresh that morning from the coast, Coyote could only taste loss.

THE BRIGHT BEAUTY
OF THE WORLD

IT WAS A WARM SUMMER EVENING after a rainstorm. The sun had come out from behind black clouds and the air was clear and the light was soft and golden. Coyote was sitting in a corner bar, staring through a gin-and-tonic at the sunset.

Lynx, the bar's beautiful cocktail waitress, was standing beside him, leaning back against her station. The bartender was off getting ice. The other two customers in the place were watching TV at the far end of the bar.

"Did you ever notice," Coyote said to Lynx, "that the world looks more blue through a gin-and-tonic?"

Lynx looked at him and shrugged. "You should see what it looks like through five or six of them," she said.

"I'm serious," said Coyote. "Things look blue. The sky looks more blue. Trees look blue-green." He held his drink to his forehead and stared at her through it. "You even look a little blue."

"No," said Lynx. "I'm a cocktail waitress. Cocktail waitresses never look blue. It cuts into their tips." She smiled at him, but then walked away and began to light the candles on the tables. Coyote continued to look at her through his glass. Lynx looked good in blue.

He had stopped in earlier than usual, knowing it was her day to work the afternoon shift. He had known, too, that the bar would empty out when the rain quit and she would have time to talk to him. And he had known, finally, that she would probably be in a foul mood because she would rather be outside in the sun instead of working a slow shift in a dark bar, at the mercy of anyone with a few bucks in his pocket and an urge to talk.

Coyote had become a regular customer because he liked to look at Lynx and watch her move. If she felt like talking that was fine, too, because she had a voice that went well with the rest of her. Coyote could listen to the beautiful sounds she made and watch the play of her lips and teeth and tongue all night long. There were nights when he couldn't remember what she said, but he never forgot the way she'd said it.

When the bartender would put drinks on Lynx's tray, Coyote would watch her take them to a table. He liked the oiled grace of her walk and the purring sound of her laugh. He even liked the cheerful detached way she dealt with the salesmen who stayed in the motel down the street, who would come in after the six o'clock news, having called their wives and put on clean beltless slacks and new shirts. They would order a drink and ask Lynx where a good place to eat was. Then, seeing her and feeling the solid comfortable warmth of her bar, they would forget dinner and drink themselves into a state of witless and self-assured charm.

Such charm eventually degenerated to pleading. Usually it was for Lynx to go with them back to their motel rooms, but in extreme cases, it was for Lynx to go away with them for a short but happy life lived from motel to motel and restaurant to restaurant until somebody back at the home office cut off the expense account credit card.

Coyote watched this and got a picture of desperate twenty-five year stints at jobs that were hated, of expense accounts padded with the righteousness of those who traded their lives for money, of bulging aortas and bad backs, of the painful crawl of clocks toward five, toward Friday, toward vacation and toward retirement. Coyote hoped that back at the motel, the jobs would seem tolerable, the wives and kids loveable, and the tradeoffs worthwhile.

As her clients grew more and more insistent, Lynx would grow more maternal and efficient and amazingly sexless, finally sending them out the door at closing time as if they were kids going off to school, giving the more favored ones a kiss on the cheek. They loved her for it. They swore eternal friendship and left her twenty-dollar tips. Lynx would clean up the tables, ask Coyote and the other regular customers at the bar to leave, and go home.

Because he had watched this ritual again and again, Coyote had gotten concerned about his own dignity when it came to cocktail waitresses. He took pains never to act like an out-of-town salesman around any of them. Never once did he even think of asking one to go home with him. He believed that as a breed they were case-hardened and apt to giggle cynically among themselves about any serious male overture. With Lynx, he was content to sit on the stool beside her station and drink in her beauty. It had begun to go well with gin.

Thus it was with practiced restraint that Coyote responded to Lynx when she returned to her station, put down a load of dirty glasses, and asked, "Do you ever get restless?"

"Restless?" asked Coyote.

"Restless," said Lynx. "Sometimes when I drive home after we've closed just want to keep on driving. It doesn't matter where. Just the sound of the wind and the sight of white lines disappearing under the hood and being alone— that's enough."

"You would have to stop for gas sometime."

"That's part of it. Stopping for gas in strange towns just as it gets light, driving around until you find a station that's open, looking at yourself in the mirror of some dirty restroom and knowing that you're on the road. I think about that when I drive home at night."

"So why not go?" asked Coyote.

She ignored him.

"Or maybe a sailboat," she said. "One sitting in a little marina somewhere. Her owner takes her out on short cruises on Sundays. He doesn't sail her out of sight of land but he won't sell her to someone who would. I'd take her around the world."

"You've got the boat all picked out?"

"Don't be so literal," said Lynx. "I made it up, owner and all. But I'm sure there's a perfect boat somewhere with an owner who never uses it. People buy toys all the time and never use them. My husband.." She paused.

Coyote looked up from his drink. He had heard she had a husband but hadn't believed it.

"My husband bought a snowmobile three years ago and it's still sitting brand new in the garage. He's used it three days."

"Maybe you can talk him into buying you a sailboat," said Coyote.

"It's five hundred miles to the ocean," said Lynx. "He tries to be practical. He bought me a car instead."

"That was a risky move," said Coyote, thinking of suddenly-blessed mirrors in dirty restrooms.

Some customers came in and she went to their table to take their order. When she returned she said, "I really think there's something wrong with me. My husband loves me. My kids get on the honor roll. Our home is full of Sears' Best. But I could disappear. I really could. You could come in here next week and ask where I was and all anybody'd say is, 'I don't know. She's disappeared. They're hunting for her in nine states.'"

"There's nothing wrong with you," said Coyote.

"You're sweet," she said, and kissed him on the cheek.

The bar became busy. Coyote sat and drank and waited for things to calm down so he could hear what Lynx had to say next, but people continued to come in all night. He ended up drinking too much. Near closing time he attempted a trip to the restroom but got his foot entangled in his barstool and fell headlong onto the plastic bucket that Lynx kept under her station. It was full of used straws and bar napkins and martini olives and half-chewed maraschino cherries. Most of them ended up in his hair and the rest went across the floor.

"What did you mean?" he asked Lynx as she picked a lemon twist off the top of his ear. "What did you mean, 'restless?'"

"Not a thing," she said. She gave him a glorious and sanitary smile, and said, "I think it must be your bedtime," and told him to wait by the door while she called him a taxi.

When he got to the door he pushed through it and walked out into the night and pissed, with as much dignity as he could muster, on the sidewalk. He found his car, got into it, fumbled for his keys and put them unsteadily into the ignition. He drove slowly down the deserted street, through a red light and onto the highway that was the main street of town. When he reached the road that turned off to his house he kept going. He centered his car over the the white lines and watched as each one rose briefly in his headlights and disappeared. He looked for himself in the rear view mirror but the green light thrown off by the instrument panel was too dim for him to see anything. "Restless," he said, but the word disappeared into the whistling of the wind.

An hour later he felt the first ragged edges of hangover. The whine of his car's old bearings began to recall suppressed memories of dentists' drills. He drove unsteadily, without destination, his movement marked by the white lines, slow weaves to and from the gravel on the road shoulder, and the distant star-like crawl of mercury-vapor lights above farmyards.

And Lynx restless was different from Lynx content. Lynx content was married. Lynx restless was less so. Coyote didn't know if that meant a rise or fall in the amount of good news in the universe.

Anyway, he could see how she might get restless. He wondered how she reconciled her reflection in the back-bar mirror with a daytime role as a tired housewife with sitters to hire, clothes to wash, *Donahue* to watch, a husband to love.

He had decided she couldn't do it. Her nighttime beauty must have seemed, in her sunlit marriage, to be an unused asset, like excess cash in a no- interest checking account.

He shrugged in the darkness. Lynx's marital condition probably didn't need that much analysis. He lived in a town of divorced or divorcing couples and there were times when he thought the operating principle in love was akin to nuclear fission: you went along accumulating beautiful memories and houses, cars, and kids until one day it all reached critical mass. Then what had appeared stable and benign began dividing and dividing again, releasing heat and blinding light and fallout that lasted for generations. It was nobody's fault, just the nature of the material.

He sighed, remembering relationships that had failed for less scientific reasons. One lover had found him in her bed with a car hop from the local root beer stand, Coyote having been seduced by the sound of the girl's voice as it asked for his order through the outside speaker. One had been pulled away by her family's money and married off, by the same mechanism, to the socially prominent owner of a sod farm. Coyote still got passionate letters from her, proposing trysts somewhere where the grass was long and unkempt and the trees gave bushy cover.

One had bought a backpack and was still, years later, camping somewhere in the nearby mountains, stealing picnic baskets and terrifying Boy Scouts with banshee screams on moonlit nights. One had made the awful mistake of talking baby talk in bed. A good many others had suggested that when Coyote had grown up and was able to belong in a committed relationship, they might be interested in seeing him again.

It was not a good track record. Coyote, when he wasn't feeling glad to have survived it, was usually feeling guilty about it. Sometimes, like Lynx, he really thought something was wrong with him.

He was relieved when he saw the first hairline of light on the eastern horizon. His head ached, and he could feel every beat of his heart directly behind his eyes. He was hungry, but the thought of eggs and hash browns and ketchup made him nauseous. He had driven three hundred miles. He was on an Interstate heading east.

It was still too dark to drive without headlights when he turned onto the business loop of a small desert town. A truckstop was open. He parked his car and went in and ordered coffee and a donut from a large and cheerful waitress. She put them in front of him and looked at him with a critical eye.

"How you feeling?" she asked.

"A little rocky," said Coyote.

"You look a little rocky," she said. "Maybe even a little bouldery."

She smiled and put a foil packet containing two aspirin beside his cup. He swallowed them and stared out the window. The first light had widened to an irregular band of red and gold. On the basalt hills on the other side of the freeway, the tops of sagebrush glowed against the yet-dark ground. Beyond the hills, a far distant range of mountains stood, still in its own shadow, like a wall to the world. Coyote wondered if spirit would expand, like a gas, to fill whatever space it found itself in.

"Nice place you've got here," he said to the waitresss as she refilled his coffee.

She looked at him suspiciously. "You being sarcastic?"

"Not at all. I was admiring your sunrise."

"It's like that almost every morning," she said, pleased.

"You like living here?" Coyote pointed out at the sagebrush desert.

"I'm not here because I like working in this goddam truck-stop," she said.

You would have to learn to love sagebrush, Coyote thought as she turned her back. You could learn to love the small grasses that grew under the short brittle branches and grey leaves. You could love the old rocks for their half-remembered shapes. Loving the spaces and the sunrises would be easy. Maybe, if you had enough water to spare, you could grow a tree.

He finished his donut. He paid the waitress and smiled his thanks at her. She asked if he was feeling better. He said he was. She told him to have a nice day. He said he bet she said that to all the guys. She said only to the ones whose heads hurt.

Outside, he filled his car with gas from the self-service pump and put in a quart of oil from the case he kept in the trunk. He washed the night's bugs off the windshield. He pulled back onto the Interstate, still heading east in the rising light. The rock along the roadside turned red, and took shape as bluffs and canyons. What green there was grew soft and dusty against the solid red of the rock. The sky became ever more blue.

A little before eight he turned off at another truckstop and pulled up to the pay phone in front of it. He dialed Lynx's number and dumped in a fistful of quarters. The phone rang seven times before a male voice answered. Coyote asked for Lynx.

"Oh, Christ," said the voice. "Don't you guys ever give up?"

There was a minute's pause, and then Lynx said, "Who is it?" Sleep and irritation were heavy in her voice.

"I drove all night," said Coyote. He had been intending to tell her about the bright beauty of the world that morning, but the words he had been saving were gone.

"You should have come with me," was all he was able to say.

VISITING RABBIT

AT DUSK, twenty hours and a thousand miles from home, Coyote drove over a rise in the Interstate and looked down on a great and shadowed city. Its streets were outlined in red by the taillights of cars. Here and there sodium-vapor lights had come on, sharpening the shapes of car lots, theme restaurants, chain-link fences and thin, newly planted trees in first-summer leaf. In the still-healing subdivisions on the city's outskirts, a hundred thousand grey roofs gave the earth a tiled look.

A hundred years before, the city's founders had chosen a sheltered fertile plain between two ranges of mountains for their home. They had dammed the mountain streams, dug canals, plowed up the sagebrush, built their houses and farms and churches. They had mined the mountains and for a while the air between the two ranges had been filled with the toxic smoke of smelters.

Things had changed. Where there had been a checkerboard network of farms there was a grid of asphalt and power lines. Canals had been roofed over and now served as sewers. The mines had given out. Fumes and smoke still hung above the ruins of abandoned smelters, but they came now from internal combustion engines and backyard barbecues, and a coal-fired plant that sat on the mountainside above the city like a huge pulsating temple to the Fire God.

Coyote turned his car off the freeway and into a rest area on a small hill that overlooked the city. He got out and walked to a fence where he could watch the sun, huge and bloodied by fifty miles of haze, approach re-entry somewhere west of the Rockies. Below him something was living and growing in a giant basin-and-range petri dish. It gave off gasses and was faintly luminescent. Could the earth in these parts have caught a disease?

He did not like the feeling of alienation that came with the question. These are your people, he said to himself. This is your civilization. Your culture.

It did no good. He was too tired and had driven too far through desert to get to this hilltop. Set free from his own century by the aged and wind- twisted landscape he had driven through, he had gone right past exits that led to Big Macs, subsisting instead on a warm half-gallon of Pepsi and a bag of chocolate-covered peanuts he had found buried in his trunk. He had driven past a distant baseball diamond at the edge of a small farming town and had not dreamed of playing shortstop for the New York Yankees but had instead lapsed into madness, imagining the Chicago Cubs in the World Series. He had not worried about getting a job, and as a corollary to this had not thought all his troubles would be over if only he had enough money. In short, he had become thoroughly lost to that civilization which had once claimed him and when he looked down on the city and saw as its paradigm colonial bacteria spreading over a smooth agar surface, all he could finally softly say was that some bacteria were more cultured than others.

He got back into his car and drove down into the haze. He turned off on one of the city's middle exits and a dozen blocks later stopped at a 7-11 store and used the pay phone stuck to its outside wall. Then he got back into his car, retraced his path onto the freeway, took another exit ten miles away, and spent the next hour driving around dark streets, peering at street signs. Finally he stopped.

He was in front of a neat small house in one of the older residential areas of town. He got out of his car, walked across the grass to the brightly lit porch, and knocked on the front door. There was a movement behind the curtains, then a rattling of chains and sliding of dead-bolts. The door opened.

"Rabbit," said Coyote.

She smiled, and in spite of what he must have looked and smelled like, she kissed him on the lips and led him into her home.

"You're lucky," she said.

"You're between boyfriends?"

"Better than that. Between husbands. Between relationships. Somewhere between life and death, if you believe my women's magazines. Anyway, you picked a good time to show up. I can't believe you drove all that way."

"Neither can I," said Coyote. He walked over to her living room couch and fell down on it.

"I think my bed might be more comfortable," she said, hesitant, but by then he was almost asleep. He vaguely felt her soft hands cover him with a knitted afghan.

He recognized its texture. It had once been promised as a gift for him, but its myriad small knots had made uncomfortable symbols. He had refused it, along with Rabbit's proposal of marriage. She had not taken either refusal well.

Sleep put a stop to this line of thought. For awhile he was aware of the sound of water running into a bathtub. Then she was shaking him awake, leading him toward the bathroom, pulling off his clothes, and helping him, sleep-stupid and compliant, into the warm water.

He fell asleep again but she woke him up before the water got cold. When he had toweled dry he walked into her bedroom, saw that the sheets on his side of the bed were turned down, and got in.

"You can go to sleep now," said Rabbit. She was reading a magazine and she concentrated on it, ignoring him. He closed his eyes and slept. Somewhere in the middle of the night he awoke and they made love, with Coyote unsure of where he was and who he was with.

When he woke, it was late morning. Rabbit had gone to to work, high up—he knew from a Christmas letter—in one of the big buildings of the city, built by a defense contractor to house its offices. Rabbit had started in one of its divisions as a secretary and had been promoted into a titled position.

He found a bathrobe laid out for him on the foot of the bed. In the kitchen a thermos of coffee was on the table, along with a note that gave explicit directions, including a map, for their noon meeting outside a downtown restaurant. He found his clothes and put them in Rabbit's washing machine, catching himself in the act of looking for its quarter slot out of long laundromat habit.

Rabbit had done well for herself. She had furnished the house, by the looks of it, from shops that called themselves galleries. The night before he had parked in her driveway beside a Japanese sports car which had cost more than he had made in any one year of his life.

Coyote smiled. When he had known her before she had been dressing in baggy old military clothes, a child born too late for the sixties but one determined to make the seventies do. She had acquired him in the same spirit she had acquired an extensive collection of worn Grateful Dead, Jefferson Airplane and Doors albums—as a relic from the Viet Nam War, one with an inexhaustable supply of old olive-drab clothes and vague memories of Hendrix live.

He, in his turn, had been drawn to a face innocent of makeup, a brow innocent of worry, a mind innocent of any evil beyond a belief that the CIA routinely assassinated rock stars, and a body that, under the fatigue jacket and oversized shirt and pants, seemed perfect and untouched. He had smiled on the plastic garbage she had brought home and hung on the walls, the art prints with brush marks molded into the paper, the beads and feather jewelry, the macrame', and the hubcap mandalas. When she discovered acid he had smiled on that too, but had refused to do it with her out of fear of his own beaten-back memories. He had finally answered her pestering questions about his war experience by telling her of a slow walk through a pacified village.

She had never asked again.

At the time, he had not recognized the poverty of spirit that came with innocence. But when she had suggested making their little world last forever, he began to feel as if he had walked into an ambush. He recognized that in allowing himself to view things the way she did, he had given her too much power, and it was the tyrannical power of a spoiled confident child over a self-doubtful adult. He had told her it was time for her to go out and see how stories ended. When she wouldn't leave, he had gone away himself.

But he had gone to her college graduation a few years later and since then they had traded letters once a year. He wondered why she hadn't told him about a husband but he supposed there were plenty of things you didn't think would be important to old lovers. That must have been one of them.

Now, in Rabbit's house, he slept between satin sheets. The brush marks on her paintings were real. Her kitchen had been extensively remodeled, with restaurant-grade fittings and appliances. A shelf of gourmet cookbooks hung above one counter. Looking into her refrigerator made him wonder if she hadn't just held up a delicatessen.

He made an awkward breakfast of croissants and eggs, thankful for the predictability of the eggs. He did bad things to the croissants, trying to make them behave like Eddy's white bread.

When he had taken his clothes from the dryer and dressed he looked at himself in the full-length mirror on the wall by the front door. With a shock, he realized he wasn't going to fit in at the ersatz noun-and-noun English pub in the basement of the office building where he was supposed to meet Rabbit. He locked the house and drove around until he found a shopping mall with a Kmart in it.

He parked his car in the parking lot and noted its location carefully. The lot was huge. Planted in corn and properly tended, as he supposed it once had been, it could have fed a good percentage of sub-Saharans.

Inside, he went looking for city clothes. He spotted a sign over the clothing section a hundred yards away and used a mountain-bred sense of direction to navigate toward it, walking down dark canyons of foreign-made running shoes, rubber boots, power tools, portable stereos, shower curtains, tennis rackets—all the goods necessary for the generic good life lived in the city's sub-urbs. Somewhere across the bulge of the Pacific, young girls were choking on carcinogenic plastic volatiles in order to provide these things. The K in Kmart stood for Korea.

Oh well. A note of cheer. Polyester was back. Coyote had read about it in a magazine. Designers had recognized its rich, waxy feel, its potential for bright contrasting colors, and had decided it had been unfairly maligned the first time around.

He picked out a shirt and slacks he hoped would serve for other urban functions he could think of—job interviews and funerals—and headed back toward the checkout stand. When he had paid he walked past the cop at the door defiantly, showing his packaged and receipted clothes like a first-class ticket. This was in contrast to other times in other Kmarts when he had gone in and had panicked before he could buy anything and had been forced to walk by exit security with a sick guilty smile on his face, prepared to turn his pockets out in an instant if challenged.

He found his car, changed into his new clothes in it, and drove off toward the center of the city. He tossed Rabbit's map away as soon as he spotted the looming shape of the building she had directed him to, and navigated through the city in the same way he had made his way the Kmart. He had occasional nasty ex-periences on one-way streets.

He was lucky for the second time on his trip. He found a park-ing space near the restaurant. He had just put two hours' worth of quarters in the meter when Rabbit walked up to him and linked her arm through his.

"Where did you get that shirt?" she asked. "You look like a refugee from Kmart."

He gave her a cold stare. "That's not funny," he said.

"I just..." she began, then understood. "Oh, my God," she laughed. "You are a refugee from Kmart. You haven't changed a bit."

The expression on his face must have moved her to mercy.

"I'm sorry," she said. "I'm used to a different type these days."

This is going to be a rough lunch, he thought to himself. Earlier, in the night, only because he had been too tired to talk or understand, it had seemed just like old times.

"What type is that?" he asked.

She started to reply, then her smile softened and she said, "There's no need for us to be unpleasant." She began to tell him about why he couldn't have met her at work.

"They give us these little plastic passes," she said, showing him hers. It had her photo and thumbprint on it, and the holographic logo of the company she worked for. They walked down a set of stairs to the entrance to the restaurant. The doorman smiled in recognition at her and waved them through. "What is it you do that requires a security clearance?" he asked her as they were shown to a table. "It's what the company does," she said. "The division I work in makes guidance systems. Another division puts them in little backpack rockets. I can't tell you what one of them would do to an airliner, but you'd be amazed."

No I wouldn't, he thought. "You've come a long way from the days you were wishing you could have been in the peace marches," he said.

"I was naive," she said. "I thought we could live in a little cabin someplace until the end of our days, living on granola, making quilts and screwing in front of the fireplace."

"You mean you can't?" asked Coyote.

"There's a real world out there. You can't ignore it." She smiled. "Anyway, the real world has its compensations. If you're anything more than a raging mediocrity, all you have to do is go to work everyday and they keep giving you more and more responsibility and money."

81

"So you can make more little rockets?"

Her nose twitched. "One of the reasons we're sitting in a restaurant instead of a bunker is because we've got lots of those little rockets. And they all go where they're pointed."

He nodded. "Good guidance systems."

"That's right. And I'll tell you something else. If it weren't for the defense industry in this state, these guys," she gestured around at the restaurant's business-suited clientele, "would be selling used cars and fire insurance to each other. Grass would be growing in the streets outside."

He supposed that was true. To the east of the city there was a huge Strategic Air Command base, to the south an area where nuclear tests had been conducted. West, they stored nerve gas. To the north—he had passed the installation driving in—there were low cinderblock buildings behind distant cyclone fences, where they worked on germs. He had no idea how much wealth all these contributed to the city's economy but he guessed it was the source which most other institutions, even this restaurant, fed on.

"Maybe I should ask you for a job," he said.

"If I thought for a moment you were serious, I'd help you," said Rabbit. "We give preference to veterans."

"I'm not serious," said Coyote.

"I know," she said. She looked at him. "I've been thinking this for a long time, but I never thought I'd have a chance to tell you. When I used to get your letters and you said you were collecting unemployment or washing dishes or helping some friend finish his house because he ran out of money to pay his contractor, I always wondered why you never got a real job, one that would mean something to you. I used to think that there a conspiracy against you. But I've realized there's no conspiracy. You don't want something like that because then you would have to start living in this world and you don't want to do that."

"I don't?"

"You don't want to ever find yourself in a position where you have to fight for something. If you lose your job dishwashing, it's no great loss. If your lover of the moment finds somebody else, it's all a joke. If somebody you know starts to work for a corporation you laugh at his suit and the car and house he buys. It all becomes trivial and unreal to you. You want to stay a moral virgin forever."

"And you were so good to me last night. Your hands were soft." He showed her a smile. "I specifically remember that your hands were soft."

"See? You can't take anything seriously. So you made the discovery it's a dirty world when you were in Viet Nam. You could have stayed home and found out the same thing. And maybe you would have had to make some decisions that had consequences and learned to live in this society well enough to become a contributing member of it."

A waiter had been quietly standing behind them. Now, while Rabbit paused for breath, he asked them if he could take their orders.

"I'll have a contributing-member-of-society burger," said Coyote, "and some napalm fries."

"See?" yelled Rabbit. "See?" She went ahead and ordered for him.

"You know what I think?" asked Coyote after the waiter had turned his back. "I don't think we have to worry about the Russians or anybody else. All we have to do is threaten to psychoanalyze them."

Surprisingly, she laughed. "I just wanted to tell you what I thought about you. But only once. I don't like to waste my time." For a moment she looked friendly. "You haven't told me how long you're planning on staying."

"Tonight," he said, making the decision quickly. "I'll be heading on in the morning."

Shadows slid into her eyes. "You must get your scripts from TV westerns," she said, but then flashed him a coquette's smile. "I guess we'll have to make a night of it, won't we?"

Their food arrived, and he began babbling a little. He told her what changes had come to their old town, what their few mutual friends had been doing, and what he planned to do in the winter if he could get enough money together in the fall. He kept up a steady impenetrable patter of light conversation, in the manner of accident survivors who throw out verbal anchors to the everyday world. When he finally let her talk, it was only to answer a question about her husband. She told him he had been her boss once, when she was a secretary. He had helped her career for awhile and then he had been transferred.

"That's an odd way to sum up a marriage," Coyote said.

"It was an odd marriage," she said.

She looked at her watch and said she had to return to work. She paid the waiter with a single large bill and she walked him to his car.

"I'll see you when I get home," said Rabbit.

He nodded. She kissed him and walked off toward her office building, her short legs making quick and efficient strides down the sidewalk. Coyote watched her until she disappeared in the crowd exiting the restaurant.

He sat for awhile in his car, trying to reconcile the untouched and waiflike presence of Rabbit in his memory with what he had just seen and heard. She had delighted in small cheap things, and he supposed he had been one of those things. He had no idea what he could offer her now.

He hoped he hadn't had anything to do with what she had become. He hoped it was more likely that a decade of living in the midst of constructs—laws and buildings, federal money and microcircuits, fast cars and enemies over the horizon—had so layered her over that whatever was left of what she had been could never get out. He wondered how her world could come to be more real for her than the one of sandstone ruins and and space and solitude he had driven through on his way to see her.

He thought again of the petri-dish metaphor that had struck him when he had first seen the city. Perhaps some pathologist-god was even now looking down and observing the colony, gauging when the products of its activity would reach toxic levels. What did you do as a solitary individual of a social species? Could you find your own spot on the petri dish and defend it against the mass? Ants, captured away from the hive, lost the meaning in their lives, moped around for a few days, and died. Maybe Rabbit was telling him to save himself before it was too late.

It seemed a good idea to get back on the road. He began driving down the street, found a freeway entrance sign, and was on his way into the desert when he remembered he had Rabbit's extra set of keys in his pocket. He thought of mailing them to her, then realized he had time enough to leave them in her mailbox with a note before she got off work. It was the sure and civilized thing to do. He found an off-ramp and within a short while he was again in front of Rabbit's house. He dropped the keys in the mailbox. On a notepad that was attached to the doorframe, he wrote I HAD TO LEAVE. WILL CALL YOU WHEN I GET TO A PHONE. It would be a phone a long way down the road.

He thought he might spend the night sleeping in his car in some red-rock canyon if he could find one that was far away enough. If he could, he would get to it about dark, driving up some rutted and disused road until he could go no further. He would open the doors to the wind and the chill of the night, would watch the forever distant stars through the windshield, and would listen for the small sounds of wind-falling sand. The first light of morning would show a different and ancient world.

He began to walk back across the neat lawn to his car, but stopped in the middle of it. "Oh, what the hell," he said. He turned around, retrieved the keys from the mailbox, went in, turned the TV to a cable news station and sat down in front of it. He was still there, eating croissants dipped in peanut butter and going around the world every thirty minutes, when Rabbit got home.

COYOTE IN LOVE

WHEN HIS FRIEND BEAR, the attorney, moved back to town, Coyote was working nights, running a dishwasher in a restaurant that catered to skiers. It was a good job. It would end when the snow melted. It would make Coyote eligible for unemployment insurance.

Bear had kept up a Christmas correspondence with Coyote since he had left for law school, sending Coyote a card imprinted with a glossy photo every late November. Coyote had always replied with a letter in January or February, telling about his job for the winter and his plans for a spring trip to someplace warm with a beach.

Over time, Bear's cards had pictured Bear himself, Bear with a sports car, Bear with the car and a wife, Bear with the wife and child and a Buick station wagon. The most recent showed Bear in front of his law offices, along with his wife, two children, and his firm's limousine.

Coyote was in the kitchen of the restaurant when Bear found him. He was pushing racks of plates and glasses into the dishwasher. Bear tapped him on the shoulder.

"Bear," said Coyote.

"They told me I could find you here," said Bear. "Surprised to see me?"

"I figured something was in the wind when I didn't get your card."

Bear grinned. "Big things in a high wind. I've moved up from L.A. Bought a condo. Got a divorce."

Coyote nodded. Bear had gained some weight and a few lines around his eyes, but he looked healthier than his last Christmas Card picture, and pleased with himself. Maybe divorce did this for you.

"It's a very nice condo," said Bear.

Coyote nodded again. "What are you going to do?"

Bear shrugged. "I have to fly back now and then to make a little money. Other than that, I'm going to enjoy life. Relax. Have fun. Do the things I never had time to do when I was working full time." He clapped Coyote on the shoulder. "All those years I envied you, you know."

"Me?"

"You kept stopping by my office on your way to Mexico. I'd be working on an important case and you would come in and tell me where you were going and what you were going to do. It was all I could do to keep from following you, chucking it all then and there." Bear paused.

"You never did," said Coyote.

"Not then." Bear sighed. "I stayed in, made money, made babies, made things much more complicated. It took a lot of untangling to get me here."

"We're a long way from Mexico," said Coyote.

"But we can go there whenever we feel like it," said Bear.

Bear left the kitchen, telling Coyote he would meet him in the restaurant bar as soon as Coyote's shift ended. Coyote returned to the dishwasher and pushed racks of glasses through the stainless steel tunnel of the machine, watching as each was snagged by little hooks on a conveyor belt, was dragged through soaping and rinsing jets, and was finally thrust out into the world again, clean and glistening. Possibly the legal system worked in a similar fashion. Bear could have hooked his life up to the conveyor of domestic justice, watched as the soapy jets swished out the detritus of wife, kids, and job, and smiled as the rinsing jets washed away the faint legal aftertaste. Bear's life would have ended up empty and sparkling, ready to be filled with something of higher proof, with more bubbles.

Running a dishwasher could be a very purifying experience, thought Coyote.

Coyote was struck with a sudden worry. Bear couldn't have made all these changes in his life just because some unemployed old friend had danced past the legal secretaries and dragged him out for a burrito and margarita at a nearby Mexican restaurant. Could he? Maybe it was all the lies Coyote had told about the Yucatan sun and beach and night life.

Coyote remembered the axiom about saving someone's life. You were responsible for what that person did from that point on, even if it was molesting Boy Scouts and small pets. If Coyote's trips had been the catalyst in Bear's life that Bear seemed to be saying they were, Bear's children were running around with latchkeys tied to their necks because of Coyote.

Thinking further, Coyote decided his own life wasn't anything to be envied or copied anyway. There had been times when he had gently touched the smooth pages of the BMW ads in news magazines, knowing that that touching was as close as he would ever get to a kind of smug, unconscious, financially-based comfort.

He finished up his shift in a foul mood, determined to tell Bear the trips to Mexico had been marked by dysentery, paralyzing fear of the local police, and deathwish hangovers. Seasonal dishwashing jobs didn't make you rich. Coyote now and then thought about his old age, and he knew whatever conveyor he was on wasn't going to leave him gleaming and spotless at its end. He would tell Bear to go back and pick up whatever remained of his old life. Smug, unconscious, financially-based comfort was better than no comfort at all.

He walked out of the kitchen and into the bar. Bear was sitting at a table in the center of the room. A blonde in a fur coat was sitting next to him. Bear called Coyote's name and waved him over. The blonde turned around to look. She was the most beautiful creature Coyote had ever seen.

"I'd like you to meet Fox," said Bear.

"I've heard so much about you," said Fox, holding out her hand. Her nails were impossibly long.

Coyote cautiously shook her hand, avoiding laceration, and smiled and nodded. He wasn't sure what to say. Fox gazed at him with piercing blue eyes. Coyote looked at Bear, who was looking at Fox. Bear, Coyote realized, was in love.

"I haven't heard a thing about you," Coyote said to Fox.

"I'm supposed to be a surprise," she said.

"A pleasant one," said Coyote, relieved that it wasn't anything he had done that had made Bear leave his wife and kids. Bear had just fallen for someone younger and more beautiful, and was escorting her through scenes of his youth. It happened to lawyers all the time.

Coyote smiled at his own vanity. He had been quite willing to assume responsibility for Bear's flight from respectable family life. Coyote's jobs were intermittent and his existence was solitary because he saw what happened to others who made their jobs or mates into their lives. It was supposed to be good, to result in successful careers and rock-solid marriages. But it changed who you were. Coyote had been spending much of his life making sure he remained Coyote, and he had thought—incorrectly, he knew now—that Bear had wanted to become Bear.

Fox smiled at Coyote, rose from her chair, and walked toward the ladies' room in a majestic sweep of fur.

"She's beautiful," Coyote said.

"Yeah," said Bear. He frowned. "Except for her nose."

"What?"

"Her nose. It's too big. It needs to be straightened. Didn't you notice?"

"I was too busy noticing everything else. But no, I didn't notice. I'm sure we can all live with it."

"I'm paying to have it fixed," said Bear. "Then she'll be perfect."

"Fixed?" asked Coyote.

When Fox again sat down at the table, Coyote grinned at her. "What does it feel like," he asked, "to be so beautiful?"

She looked down at her drink. "I'm not beautiful," she said.

Bear cleared his throat. "We've got to be going," he said. "We just wanted to say hello."

"I just got here," said Coyote. "You haven't even bought me a drink."

"I'm not beautiful," repeated Fox, and stood up, motioning with her head toward the door. Bear took her arm, but she pulled away from him and walked a few steps away from the table.

"You shouldn't have asked her that," said Bear. "She's sensitive about how she looks to people. Just because she's beautiful doesn't mean she's not sensitive."

"I'm not beautiful," said Fox again. "Not yet." She turned to leave.

Bear waved goodbye. "I'll talk to you later," he said, and disappeared. Coyote realized he had just been expected to see her, not talk to her.

A difficult time began for Coyote. He had always assumed Bear and others like him were busy making traps for themselves. Now Bear seemed to have escaped his. Not only that, but he had ended up with Fox. Jovial and proud, Bear took her around town, showed her off after her nose job, made friendships with her at their focus, and started small businesses with her at his side.

Bear's friendship with Coyote suffered. Coyote seemed to have nothing that was of value to Bear, a change from the days of Mexico and unemployment checks. Bear had refined his career into two trips a month to Los Angeles. His partners took care of the details, he told Coyote. He was once again driving an exotic two-seat car. His condo was in an expensive neighborhood Coyote rarely frequented.

Bear collected a crowd of new friends. Afternoons, they drank in the restaurant Coyote worked in, had dinner there, and were there when Coyote joined them after his shift. The talk was about business and money, and Coyote did not join in. Bear laughed a lot. It was tempting to want to live that way.

Occasionally Coyote decided to try to talk to Fox, but he found himself unable to keep from mutely staring at her new nose. He couldn't remember what the old one had looked like, only that it must have been too large and had been somehow crooked.

Once Fox asked him about his job, and he told her as much as he could about operating the dishwasher, scraping plates, stacking glassware, and the advantages of several brands of industrial detergents. There wasn't much to tell, and she didn't seem to be interested in anything else about him. Maybe Bear had told her everything she wanted to know. Maybe, he realized, she wasn't used to dealing with anyone who didn't translate his life into the language of his job.

Just once he was able to ask her what he really wanted to know.

"What does it feel like?" he asked.

"What?"

"To have had the surgery. To look in the mirror and not see the same thing."

She looked offended. "Do you always ask tacky personal questions?"

"Just when I'm curious."

She shrugged. "It feels the same."

"As what?"

"As the others. As the tummy tuck. The implants. The depilation. The lipodectomy. For awhile you look different to yourself. Better. Then you get used to it and it feels the same."

Coyote looked at her closely. There, where her hair touched her perfect skull, were the faint beginnings of dark roots.

Everything that ever happened left traces, he thought later. Even the walls can be pieces of film and recording tape. Every time you walk through a room their molecules change a little. Sunlight and shadow, the vibrations of laughs and sighs, the exhalation of sweet moist breaths—all these were recorded, however faintly, in the chemical structure of the universe.

Somewhere there was a house where Fox had grown up, its surfaces etched with her presence. Delicate instruments would have to be designed, techniques of enhancement invented. But somewhere there was a record of what she had been.

At the end of the ski season, Bear came into the kitchen at the end of Coyote's shift. He looked older, more tired, a loser in the gravity war. He sat down heavily on a stack of empty dish racks.

"It's over," he said.

"Not yet," said Coyote. "I still have to clean the dishwasher." He shut off the conveyor belt and jets. The room filled with a quick silence and Coyote realized that he, like Bear, was tired.

"You don't understand. I'm leaving. I'm going back to L.A. I can't make enough money commuting."

"We might be able to get you a job here," said Coyote, as he pulled bleached maraschino cherries and soggy cocktail olives out of the dishwasher's clogged filter.

Bear looked irritated. "I can't keep her happy. All she talks about is the money I could be making if I was working full-time."

Coyote turned a valve and allowed the water to drain from the dishwasher. When it was empty, he refilled the soap reservoir with liquid detergent. Then he turned fresh water into the machine so it would be ready for the after-lunch shift.

"She starts crying," said Bear, "and asks me, 'Do you love me?' Of course I love her, I think to myself. 'I love you,' I say, and right then I realize I'm not sure." Bear looked glum. "She looks terrible when she's crying."

"What does she want?"

"I don't know." Bear sighed. "She says she doesn't like it here. It's the sun and the altitude and the humidity. She says they're aging her skin."

Coyote watched as clear water rose to the overflow mark on a glass window in the steel side of the dishwasher. He shut off the valve. "All done," he said.

"She's in the bar," Bear said. "Say hello to her. Maybe you can cheer her up."

But when they walked out to the bar, Fox was not there.

"She must have gone out to the car," said Bear. "She was upset." He went out the door to look for her in the parking lot.

Fox came out of the ladies' room and sat down beside Coyote, who had ordered a beer. She looked as beautiful as ever.

"I wish I had enough money to get a face-lift," she said.

"Bear's out there looking for you," said Coyote, pointing toward the door. "You better go with him."

She gave him a sad smile and walked away from him forever.

Bear sold his condo and went back to Los Angeles. In subsequent years, Coyote waited for Bear's Christmas Cards and scanned them for news of Fox. Bear had married her, and there were children. Bear got older in the Christmas pictures and one year he went noticeably grey, but he always had the look of someone making lots of money. Fox photographed well.

Coyote always scrutinized the pictures to see if it was really her wishing him Merry Christmas. She had, he thought, gotten her facelift. One year she had acquired a dimple. During another her cheekbones had risen. Her breasts had one year become girlish. Her hair waved and bobbed with current Los Angeles fashion. Her contact lenses went from blue to violet to an electric green.

Coyote replied to the cards with a letter about his life and job, but he never mentioned where he was going in the spring, nor did he charge into Bear's office on his way. In a small way he envied Bear, and the thought of having to sit down and share a meal with Bear made him uncomfortable.

If you could sense the mystery in someone else, be intrigued by it and go after it and yet never be quite able to touch it or understand it—that could make up for a lot of routine writing of briefs or arguing before a jury. Coyote supposed Bear was happy.

On the beaches, Coyote would lie in the sun for a few days until the tension instilled by a winter's worth of cold would leave his body. Then, staggering a little from sunburn and tequila, he would take long walks along the wave–edge, looking among the beauties on the beach for someone exactly like Fox.

COYOTE IN
THE MOUNTAINS

WHEN COYOTE HAD FIRST GLIMPSED the fish, it had been a bright flash in the center of the pool. As his shadow fell upon the surface of the water, the fish had darted beneath the bank on the far side.

Coyote crossed the stream on a log below the pool. He walked to where he had last seen the fish and reached into the water and under the overhang of bank. He moved slowly until he felt the faint rhythms of fins and tail against water. Then he touched fish belly and moved gently up to gill plates.

You weren't secure out there in the middle of the pool, he thought. It feels safer for you—you're a fish, it's just your nature—to be in under the bank, where it's dark. There's a lesson for us all here somewhere.

In one smooth motion, Coyote grabbed the fish in under the gills and flung it out of the water. It danced madly in the dry dirt and duff of the streambank until Coyote caught it again and clubbed its head against a rock. It stiffened and died. Coyote looked into its clouding eye and saw a little fish-spirit leaping among the rocks and trees of the mountainside, falling down the waterfalls of light that cascaded off peaks, resting in the deep pools of valleys.

He reached in his pack for a knife and gutted the fish. When he finished he threw the entrails back in the bushes—there were others that were hungry— and washed the blood and dirt off the fish and himself. He built a small hot fire, then pulled a piece of aluminum foil from his pack, wrapped the fish in it and threw it onto the flames. When the fire had burned down to a pile of coals, Coyote picked up one end of the foil, unwrapped the golden–pink flesh, and ate.

A little later he continued up the stream. It ran between two lakes in a glacier-carved valley, and its water poured over polished rock into deep pools, riffled out of them and fell into pools below.

The trail connecting the lakes did not follow the stream. As he climbed over fallen logs and through bushes, he caught occasional glimpses of the thin scar on the other side of the valley, and of the bright-colored specks of backpacks moving up it. At the upper lake, where they were headed, there were campsites. They would all be full tonight. Coyote, who sometimes camped on ridges, had looked down into valleys during the night and had seen the outlines of lakes marked bright by lines of campfires.

He no longer visited lakes on his trips into the mountains. Too many campers had made them their destinations. Along shorelines, feet had eroded the ground vegetation away, leaving only the dry hard dirt and the grey dust of old fires. The bark of trees had been worn smooth by too many leaning backs or shoulders. Firewood was scarce, and most trees had lost their lower branches. Things had been touched too much at the lakes.

As he got near the upper lake, he left the stream and climbed up the wall of the valley. He looked for pockets of rock crystal as he climbed, checking the cavities and cracks in the granite for the glint of dark crystal faces.

The mountains he was standing in had once been five miles down in the earth. Their rock, still almost molten, had been filled with bubbles and fissures, and these had filled with superheated water. Silica had dissolved out of the rock and into the water. Later, as the mountains had risen toward the surface and cooled, the silica had precipitated out as crystals of quartz. Somewhere down there radioactivity had been intense enough to turn the crystals black—it altered them on an atomic level, and they turned from clear prisms to dark mirrors.

It had taken millions of years, Coyote knew, for the gigantic block of rock to float upward through the soft crust of the earth and become the mountains he was in. Once it had pushed through, glaciers had chewed its high spots into the sharp horns of peaks and had smoothed its crevices into gentle U-shaped valleys. When he walked over the bare rock, he could see the marks of the glacier's movement. Here and there deep channels had been cut by chunks of broken rock carried along the glacier's underside.

Too much force, he thought, to really understand what happened. That, and too much time. He could only touch the hard smoothness of the granite, only see in its fluted surface the final evidence of the glacier's weight. It would take thousands of Coyote-lifetimes to see that the rock was softer than it seemed, was a plastic and changeable thing.

He began climbing up a narrow chute to the top of the ridge that separated the valley he was in from the next. It was steep, but he could see a way to the top of it and knew he would have no trouble getting there.

There were routes in the mountains he had climbed when he was young, but now he could no longer travel up or down them. The leaps of faith they required were over too much air. He had once started down a rock face he had been up and down a dozen times, but had been stopped by the terror of a three-hundred-foot drop, a slanted ledge, loose rock and sand underfoot. The mountains must have changed, he had thought then, or someone else had gone across the ledge. This was what had happened to him as he had grown older—he had begun to lose the connection with the selves he had been.

He found a small crystal on his way up the chute. It had been lying in the sunlight, and was bleached and clear. The light of day annealed the crystals, healed whatever damage radioactivity had done. Over time they grew lighter, to a golden brown, then white and transparent, as if they stored the sunlight as it struck them. It was impossible not to attach moral significance to the process.

Coyote smiled. He much preferred the black ones. You had

to hold them up to the sun to see through them, and the faint feathers and fractures inside them—accidents of a long distant birth—were like deep dreams.

He remembered finding pockets of crystals, reaching back in and drawing them forth, scraping away the soft clay that covered their sides. Nothing had ever seen them before. Of all the creatures who grasped and held glittering things up to the light, he was the first.

He held the crystal like a talisman, hoping it would help him find the path to its brothers. It didn't. He reached the spine of the ridge without finding anything but broken granite and sand.

He looked down into the next valley. He could see six lakes. Smoke was already rising from campfires around them. He left the crystal on top a flat rock, and for awhile watched it as it hovered in the current of the late afternoon sun.

Then he began to slowly dance down the boulders on the ridge, feeling the sun warm his shoulders, happy that for this moment at least, Coyote-time and the time of the world were the same.

About the Author

John Rember grew up along the Salmon River in Sawtooth Valley, Idaho, and recently has returned there to live. He has an M.F.A. in fiction from the University of Montana, and works as a freelance writer. *Coyote in the Mountains* is his first book.

About the Artist

Julie Scott lives in Ketchum, Idaho, where she makes her way as a painter and as a graphic designer/illustrator for national magazines.

COLOPHON

Coyote in the Mountains comprises No. 21 of *The Limberlost Review*. The design of this book was done by Julie Scott. Layout and typesetting was done by Jerry Poyser on computer using Xerox Ventura Publisher and output to a Linotronic 100 phototypesetter. The types are Trump Medieval and Kabel. Twenty-six copies of the first edition have been lettered A-Z and signed by author and artist.